Facing the Bull-Y

The Adventures of Silver Dove, Book Six

Eliza Scalia

Cover Illustration by: Wayne F. Shurtz and
Cheyanne and Jean Buffkin
Based upon the characters originally
designed by Suji Gallianetti

Copyright © **2020 Eliza Scalia**

Published by: Winged Publications

ISBN-13: 978-1-952661-13-6

Dedicated to a specific bully I had in school. I have recently learned that he has passed away. May his life after death be better than his life on earth, for I knew he had great pain. My experiences with him helped inspire the character Alex, as well as many others for stories I will tell later. Although we may not have been friends, I still wish you well.

Chapter One
Colomba-
Sophomores Now

There is a bit of a chill in the air as I make my way through the front doors of my school, Drew's Hollow High. I wrap my scarf tighter around my neck as I walk through the crowd of other students wandering through the halls. The new school year started about a month ago and I still feel excited knowing that I am now a sophomore.

I am walking to my first class with my two best friends, Nat and Luis. The three of us are laughing joyfully at a joke Luis just said and, for a moment, it almost feels as if I don't have a care in the world. I know that's a lie though. I have more to worry about than most people. I have to worry about some lunatic with superpowers who calls himself the Crow. I have to make sure that whenever he pops up that I have to stop him as Silver Dove to make sure that he doesn't hurt anybody. Yeah, most people don't have to worry about crazy stuff like that. A lot of people my age complain about being bored, but I would rather be bored sometimes than deal with some of the weirdness I go through regularly. I mean seriously, just having one weekend without having to do some kind of flying, fighting, or sword training with my grandmother would really be nice. I glance over to the side to see another person I have to worry about, Alex.

Alex glances over at me and it looks like he is about to walk over to try and talk to me, but I turn my gaze away from him, clearly showing that I do not want him near me. Last year we were pretty good friends, but not anymore. I finally listened to the advice that multiple people had given me about getting away from him after I saw him act meanly toward Luis. If someone is mean to one of my friends, then I will not be friends with them. It is a bit painful knowing that I am hurting Alex's feelings by not even letting him come near me, but I can't keep making the mistake of letting him stay in my life. It wouldn't be fair to my friends and it wouldn't be fair to me.

I finally made the decision to kick him out of my life when he was being mean to Luis at the fair over a month ago by trying to make him look weak and embarrassing him. While we were there the Crow came back after a few months' vacation, and I had to fight his newest victim, the Beauty Queen. That was a good day for Luis too since he won several county fair ribbons for his artwork. He even got first prize for a portrait he did of me. I was so proud of him. That really seems to have helped him, he is a lot more confident than he used to be. He still has a lot of trouble speaking to people that he doesn't know, but whenever he is around me and any of my other friends he is smiling and speaks his mind. It has been so nice to watch him grow over the past year. I can only hope that he will continue to grow and won't be brought back down again.

Due to my great grades last year, I am placed in all advanced classes. It took a lot of extra work to do this since I have been spending so much time training as Silver Dove and I wasn't able to study as much as I would have liked. I guess that I will have to make up for that this year. Oh well, no matter what happens I know that I will be happy and that I can make it through. No matter what has happened, I have always been able to make it through.

I glance back over at Alex to see that he is no longer looking at me, he is looking at Luis. Well, I can't really say looking, it's more like he's glaring at Luis with more hatred than anyone should ever have in them. I turn to Luis, hoping that he hasn't noticed Alex's cold glare. My hopes are completely useless. Luis is glaring right back at Alex with just as much hatred in his eyes. A chill runs down my spine at seeing that kind of hatred in the eyes of my friend. Luis is always so calm and sweet, it's almost unbelievable to see him glare at Alex with so much venom.

When I glance back and forth between the two of them, it almost feels as if they are silently challenging each other. It's as if an invisible battle is going on between them. The blood in my veins turns cold as I look at the hatred passing between their gazes. What really disturbs me about what is going on between them is that I have the unnerving feeling that this silent challenge they have between them has something to do with me. I suddenly feel queasy as a wave of guilt comes over me. I am responsible for this, I just know that I am. Thankfully, as I keep walking away from Alex, Luis walks with me. I was almost afraid that he would stay back and try to fight Alex. With the death glare he was giving him, I wouldn't be surprised. The two of us head to class, both silent as we are stuck in our own thoughts.

Chapter Two
Luis-
A New Year

When we walk in the front doors of the school, I enter with my friends smiling. This is a bit of an unusual thing for me. For most of my life I hated walking into my school because I knew that I would go through terrible stuff at the hands of the other kids around me, but this year is different. This year I am actually happy coming to school since I know that I will be with my friends. I still have to deal with a lot of people messing with me, but it doesn't seem as bad because I have some friends that I can spend time with to help get rid of some of that pain. It's better to be in pain but have people who care about you than to be in pain and be alone.

I glance down at Colomba to see that she is looking over at something that has taken the smile off her face. I look over to see what she is staring at, and the smile disappears from my face too. Alex is smiling over at her with that smug grin that he always has, but when Colomba turns away from him that smile quickly fades away to be replaced with a hurt expression. It honestly feels kind of nice to see. When Alex notices me staring at him, his glance changes to a glare that burns a hole in my soul. I know why he is so angry at me right now; it's been like this for weeks now. He's furious with me because Colomba chose me as a friend over him. She realized just how much of a monster he is, and she decided to dump him as her friend. He blames me for that and has been trying to get back at me ever since this school year started. He hasn't succeeded though. Due to Colomba's help with homework and everything, I was able to get really good grades last year and now I've been placed in mostly advanced placement classes while Alex is in the regular classes. Because of that we do not share any classes together like last year. That means that he doesn't see me very much which also means he has a hard time finding the time or opportunity to pick on me and get his revenge.

The two of us glare at each other with as much venom as we can. It almost feels as if we are daring the other to look away first. I won't back down though. He has hurt me long enough. I won't back down anymore. He has no more control over me. I know that he wants to try and get close to Colomba again, but I won't let that happen. He has been hurting me almost my entire life, I won't let him hurt her.

After what feels like ages, Alex is the one who looks away first. I smile in triumph until I look down again at Colomba to see that she is staring at me with curiosity. She obviously just saw what was going on between Alex and I, but she doesn't say anything about it as she answers a question that Nat just asked her. Man, I hope she never asks me about this ever. I don't know what I could say to explain what just happened between me and Alex.

The three of us walk to our first classes. Colomba and Nat go down one hallway and I am left alone, and the fear comes over me. I keep my gaze wandering from side to side while I keep my head down. I may be a bit more confident than I was last year, but that does not mean that all my problems are solved. As I think about this, I manage to get out of the way just in time when someone sticks their foot out in front of me to try and trip me. After so many years of having people do that to me, I have learned how to be aware and keep myself safe. I move quickly through the crowd so that they won't have time to figure out something else they can do to me.

I make it safely to my first class and sit at my desk. Even though there isn't anybody really close to me, I still keep my eyes glued to everyone in the room. I know what these people are capable of. They have hurt me countless times over the years, I know that if I let my guard down then they will strike. I must always be vigilant. I can never truly relax when I am in this school. I am never free. Until the day that I have finally won as the Crow, I will never be free.

Chapter Three
Colomba-
Amazing News

I slowly make my way through the crowded hallway, eager to get to my third period class. I always love going to this class, for one reason I have it with Luis, reason number two is that it's Advanced Art History which is pretty interesting, and three it is with a really awesome teacher, Mr. Sizemore. Luis used to tell us about him last year when he had Mr. Sizemore for art. Luis also takes a more advanced art class this year with Mr. Sizemore as well, something that Luis is very happy about. As I make my way through the crowd of people, a voice stops me dead in my tracks.

"Hey Colomba, how are you doing?" Standing right in my way is Alex. I look away from his smiling face as I give him my reply.

"Hey Alex." He either doesn't notice or doesn't care about how uncomfortable I obviously am, since he still sounds very cheerful when he speaks to me again.

"I'm glad I ran into you. Can I walk you to

class?" I finally look up at him, but I do not smile, I keep my face blank so that he will see that I don't really care if he's talking to me or not. He doesn't matter to me.

"No thanks, I'm already here." I point to the door of my classroom which is only a few feet behind him. He smiles more deeply when he looks at the door I'm indicating.

"Well what do you know, we're neighbors. My next class is right next to yours." It suddenly feels as if I just ate something bad, I want to puke. I know what this means. Since our classrooms are right next to each other he will try to talk to me in the halls when I'm heading in or going out of my classroom. Just knowing Alex, he will do this to me every day if he can. Things just got a whole lot worse for me.

"Okay, cool." I nod my head at what he said, still trying to keep my face straight when I really just want to get angry and yell at him. Why can't this guy see that I'm not interested in him? Why does he continue to pester me? I walk around him to head into my class, but Alex just walks beside me and into the classroom with me.

"I have a couple minutes until class starts, I bet your teacher won't mind if I hang out here for a bit." I'm about to tell him that *I* would mind if he tried to hang out with me again, but he continues talking. "I'm not sure if you've heard, but at the big game this Friday I'm going to be pretty much leading the team. The coach has already gone over the game plan with us the other day, and I will be on that field practically all night. Of course, he planned it that way because he knows that the team can't really get anywhere without me."

My gosh, can this guy even see past whatever's going on in his life? Is he so self-centered that he can't even see that I don't care, and I don't want him around me? Why is he even like this at all? I have never met anybody as self-centered as him before. What happened to him growing up that made him start to think that he is the greatest thing that's happened since sliced bread? Is he always treated like a prince at home or something? I don't know why he is the way he is; I just know that I don't like the results.

My angry thoughts about him are interrupted by Mr. Sizemore calling to me from his desk where Luis is already standing. Luis must have only just noticed that we arrived since his eyes grow wide when he notices Alex talking with me. He's probably worried that Alex is trying to get close to me again. He is such a good friend to worry about me like this.

I walk away from Alex to head over to Mr. Sizemore's desk, but Alex actually follows me up there. What is wrong with this guy!? Why can't he just go away? Mr. Sizemore smiles through his beard at me as I get up to his desk, his eyes sparkling in joy.

"I thought that since you were involved with this then I should tell you both the news at the same time." I glance over at Luis, but he only shrugs at me. He's just as clueless as I am.

"What kind of news is it?" I ask and Mr. Sizemore chuckles, seeing both of our confusion.

"Don't worry, it's good news. Apparently, a doctor in town saw Luis' portrait of you at the county fair and he really liked it. I had spoken to him for a bit so he heard me showing off about how I teach art to the winner, and he would like you to do another artwork that he can hang up in his waiting room. He will be happy to pay you for your work as well as pay for the tools you will need to complete your work if you are interested." My eyes stretch wide in shock. When I look over at Luis, he shares my shock. A huge smile flashes on my face as I wrap my arms around Luis in a tight embrace which he returns.

"Congratulations Luis! This is absolutely amazing!" As I hug Luis, I look over his shoulder to see Alex staring at the two of us with shock, but not the happy shock that Luis and I had a moment ago. His shock is coming from the fact that I am hugging Luis when I would barely even talk to him when he was telling me about playing in that big game. It is a shock that comes from his jealousy. He clears his throat awkwardly as Luis and I release each other from the embrace.

"Well, class is going to start any second so I'm gonna head out. I'll talk to you later Colomba." He gives me a quick smile that quickly switches to a glare that he directs at Luis before he turns away to head out of the classroom. When I look up at Luis, his expression isn't what I would have expected. I would have expected Luis to look a bit intimidated or something by Alex's glare since Alex has always seemed to frighten Luis, but that isn't even close to what he is showing on his face. More than anything,

Luis almost looks as if he is proud of himself. As if he just won a major battle against Alex that I don't even know about. What did I just miss? I don't have time to think about what just happened since I watch in happiness as Luis accepts the challenge of doing this artwork for the doctor and gets the doctor's phone number from Mr. Sizemore to get in contact with him after school. With that done, Mr. Sizemore starts the class and Luis and I take notes with smiles on our faces.

In my happiness, it only feels as if we have been in the class for a few minutes before the bell rings, signaling the end of class. As soon as I have gotten out of my chair, Luis is chatting excitedly to me. He is talking so much that I am almost tempted to laugh. I have never heard him talk so much at once. Luis talks about how surprised and excited he is about all of this, as well as his hopes that this might lead to more paid work for him to do with his art.

As we leave the classroom, I notice Alex leaning against a row of lockers. I know what he is doing. He is waiting for me so that he can try and talk with me while walking me to my next class. He is sorely disappointed though when he sees that somebody has taken his place beside me. Luis suddenly grows silent and I return my attention back to him to see that he is blushing furiously, and his long hair hangs in his face as he lowers his head in embarrassment. He glances at me through the curtain of his hair as he smiles shyly.

"Colomba, I was wondering, if you're interested, if this guy lets me paint what I want, would you model for me again? It was really fun the last time and I have something in mind for a painting. If you don't want to or are busy, then I completely understand. I don't mind at all, I'm sure I could figure something out." I smile at him, so proud that he wants to use me again for his work.

"I would love to help you. It will be so much fun." Luis' face lights up as he thanks me over and over again for my help. From the corner of my eye, I notice that Alex's charming grin that he had been directing at me has disappeared and is now a glare. He overheard what Luis and I just said, and he is not even bothering to hide his hatred toward Luis. I look away from him, afraid of the terrifying fire in his eyes. I let my mind return to the conversation I'm having with Luis. I don't want to focus on Alex again. He doesn't deserve my attention or my thoughts. What I do need to focus on is Luis and his plans for this next painting. I am excited to help him again, I had a great time the last time I did it and I'm sure that it will be just as fun, or even better, this time. I can only hope that Alex won't try and get in the way. After seeing that deep, bitter hatred in his eyes, I wouldn't be surprised if he did try to do something to ruin our work.

Chapter Four
Luis-
The Procedure

As I sit in my fourth period, I take notes but I'm not really paying attention. My mind is too busy thinking about the painting that the doctor wants me to do. I keep going over different places I can set up for the painting, what time of day I want it to be, and what kind of poses that I would like Colomba to do in the painting.

It still feels unbelievable that somebody is actually going to pay me to do a painting for them. It's also unbelievable that Colomba agreed to do this for me again. She is so sweet. I can only hope that when I give the doctor a call after school that he will agree to let me paint Colomba. I'm sure he will though. I mean, if he liked what I did at the fair so much, when it was a drawing of her, then I'm sure that he would be alright with having a painting of her.

I loved seeing the look of jealousy on Alex's face when he heard about me doing that painting and then later when Colomba was telling me that she would be happy to model for me again. It was fantastic. He will probably try to do something to me in his anger, but I will stay vigilant. I won't let the thought of him going to get me ruin the happiness I feel now.

My thoughts and the class are interrupted when an irritating siren sound goes off on the intercom and I can hear several of the other students groan in annoyance. We all know what this is by now, it is a Crow Drill. Everyone gets out of their seats to do what we have all been trained to do. During the summer, I heard the principal of our school tell people on the news that they were setting up a procedure to make sure that when the Crow shows up again that everyone will be prepared. What he has us doing though is completely stupid and I don't think anybody believes that it will work.

For this drill, all of the students have to go over to the corner of the room that's the farthest from the door and stay as quiet as possible while the teacher turns out the lights and locks the door. The teacher is doing this now for the drill and she looks really annoyed. I don't think any of the teachers think that this will work either, but they are just following the orders of their stupid boss. The principal probably doesn't think this will help either, but it will make him look good to other people since it looks like he is actually doing something. I almost want to laugh right now. Everyone is terrified of me. After spending all of my life being terrified of them, they are now terrified of me. It's beautifully ironic.

All of the students stay huddled together

like frightened kids for a couple minutes before the principal comes over the intercom to tell us that the Crow Drill is now over. Everyone starts chatting as the teacher goes over to turn on the lights and unlock the door. She tries to start the class again, but nobody is really listening anymore. The drill took all of their attention. Thankfully, the teacher doesn't get angry about this since there is only about five minutes of class left so she just tells us to not get too loud as we talk before the bell rings.

Since I don't really have anybody to talk to in this class, I start going through my mind to figure out a good place to do the painting of Colomba. I don't want to do it in her backyard again since that would just feel like doing the same thing again, and that's just plain boring. I don't know about some people, but I can't draw the same thing over and over again, it would drive me nuts from boredom. To me, that's like eating the same meal every day forever. I just can't do it.

My mind goes through countless places, trying to figure out the perfect one, while the rest of the classroom is full of the buzz of many conversations going on at once. I want to join one of the conversations, I want to tell people about how awesome it feels to be doing this painting, but I know that none of them will care. They don't care about me at all. They would just be annoyed if I tried to talk to them.

I make some sketches of what I hope the painting will look like until the bell rings and I head out of the classroom, my mind still going through what kinds of paint colors I will want to use for it.

While I think this through, my thoughts are interrupted by people cheering down the hall. I look up to see several people high fiving someone wearing a football jersey. The guy turns around and I am not surprised to see Alex looking so proud while everyone in the hallway praises him. Did he just put that on since the last time I saw him? He was wearing a regular shirt before when I saw him with Colomba. Did he just put that on so people would praise him and make himself feel better after what happened with Colomba? Wow, that is just sad… and also pretty hilarious. How pathetic can you get?

Also, what is up with everybody cheering for him? I couldn't care less about sports, but even I know that there is a big game coming up on Friday. Why are they praising him now? The guy hasn't even done anything yet and they are already praising him. This does not make any sense to me. Why are people so stupid?

As Alex makes his way through his adoring crowd, he stops for a moment and a smile creeps across his face when he sees me. My entire body has become stiff in terror because I know what that smile means. Something bad is about to happen to me. I want to try and run away, but I know that it is too crowded for me to do that and he is also much too close to me. Even though I know this, I try to maneuver my way through the crowd, but it is too late. Alex rams his shoulder into my chest and the stuff I had been holding scatters on the ground in a huge mess. Alex pretends not to notice this and steps all over my books and papers. I gather them all quickly while everyone laughs and gives Alex a few more high fives, congratulating him on how well he hurt me. My books seem pretty okay, just a little bit of mud on them from his shoes, but when I look at the sketches I had been making at the end of class of my plans for the painting, I can see that they are ruined. Mud has covered them, making the paper soggy. I close my eyes and release a sigh of defeat.

While I walk to my next class, I toss the ruined papers in the trash as I realize the obvious. This is only the beginning. Alex blames me for how things are between him and Colomba and he will do everything he can to make my life a living nightmare. I can't let that get to me though because I know the truth. I have won. Sure, he will always be there to pick on me and everything, but Colomba doesn't want anything to do with him and that's what he really wants. I have that, and he never will. I try to keep that thought alive so that I can have some light in my day as I carry my muddy books to my next class.

Chapter Five
Colomba-
Tutoring

Nat, Luis, and I are just coming out of lunch and we are heading to our next class. Nat is telling us about her weird new neighbors who apparently breed fluffy dogs and then use the dog's hair to knit sweaters… *Very* weird neighbors. As we pass by a notice board on the wall, one of the papers pinned to the board catches my eye and I stop to read it.

Would you like to make some quick cash?
Come and tutor your fellow students and earn some money for yourself.

"Hey guys, come and check this out! This sounds awesome!" Nat and Luis come over to look at the poster, but they aren't as excited about it as me.

"I don't think I would like that." Nat says as she looks at the paper. "I don't like telling people what to do and I don't want to get stuck tutoring someone I don't like." I know that what she's saying is true, but I also know that Nat doesn't want to do this since she is shy, and it would make her uncomfortable. Luis looks just as hesitant, maybe even a bit more than her.

"Yeah, I don't think that this would be my kind of thing either. I bet you would be good at it though." I smile at him, knowing that he means it.

"Thanks, I'll have to sign up for it later. I could definitely use the money. My grandmother and I are going to try and make some quilts so that we can sell them, and we could use a few bucks to get more materials." The three of us start walking again, continuing the conversation we were having before I stopped to look at the poster. When Nat is finished talking about her freaky neighbors, Luis starts talking about the painting he will do for the doctor.

"So, would after school today be a good time for you to help me start the painting?" Luis asks a little nervously.

"Sure, that sounds perfect to me." he smiles joyfully, his nervousness forgotten as he continues talking about what he hopes the painting will look like. I smile as he talks, so happy to see my friend look so excited. He really has changed so much since the time I first met him. When I first saw him, he was on the ground getting picked on by Angela and he had a hard time speaking to anybody. Now he is chatting casually with us as if this is nothing and is holding his head high. I am so proud of the change that my friend has gone through in only a year.

The rest of the school day passes rather

quickly and as the final bell rings I go to the teacher in charge of the tutoring program and get signed up before I head to my bus. As soon as I am sitting on the bus seat, I take out my cell phone to tell my dad that I won't be home until later because Luis and I are going to the park to do a painting. He is alright with that, a little confused, but alright. So instead of getting off at my stop, I leave with Luis at his uncle's shop. Apparently, they have an apartment upstairs.

We spend a few minutes talking with his uncle before he grabs some of his art stuff so that we can walk the three blocks to the town park. The sun is shining down on us as we walk, making the day look absolutely gorgeous. When we do make it to the park, I smile with joy at the sight of it.

The park is basically just a giant hill. At the top of the hill is a small playground for little children to play on. At the moment, I can see around three or four children playing on the swing set. One side of the hill is just an empty little grassy field for kids to run around on, a man is throwing a ball to his hyperactive labradoodle there now. That field is used during the summer for festivals for people to put tents on. The other side of the park, on the other side of the hill, is where Luis wants to do the painting. On that side is a small lake. The kids don't really go there to play since they aren't allowed to go in the lake and swim. It is the more peaceful part of the park that not many people visit. Most people just use the sidewalk trail around it to take a leisurely walk. Nobody really stops to admire the beauty of it, but that is what Luis is going to try and do, capture the beauty of this forgotten place.

The two of us walk around the lake a few times before Luis decides on the perfect spot. It is a secluded little spot hidden among some trees on the edge of the water. He asks me to sit on a large rock that sits halfway in the water and hallway out. I do what he says and sit down on it so that I am facing the water. I take off my shoes since, when I dangle my feet down, my toes are dipping in the water. I stare down at my toes in the water, watching the water gently ripple with each movement of my foot.

"That's perfect, keep that position." Luis says enthusiastically as he goes over to my right so that he can draw me from the side. I do as he says and keep my head down to stare at the water. From the side, I can hear Luis' pencil quickly flying across his sketchpad. He says that he wants to make a sketch of what he wants to paint first so that he can figure out how he wants it to come out, or something like that. I don't really know much about painting or art, so I let him do whatever he feels like he needs to do. He gets so focused on his work that he barely says a word, but I don't mind. It is kind of nice to see him so wrapped up in his work. The two of us stay in silence as the breeze gently blows through the trees around us, making the world seem completely at peace.

Chapter Six
Luis-
The Ambush

I walk with a skip in my step as I walk away from the curb where Colomba's grandmother's car was a moment ago. She just picked her up after our first painting session right in front of the park. I carry all my art stuff with me as I head down the street to head to my Uncle Diego's shop. My feet splash in a few puddles that I walk through that were created earlier today by a quick rain shower that happened sometime around lunch.

The smile I have is so big that my face feels a bit sore from holding that smile for so long. It's kind of like when someone is taking forever to take your picture and you have to hold that smile for what feels like a million years, that's what it feels like. I don't care though. I'm too happy to really care about anything. Why shouldn't I be happy? I was just in the park, hanging out with the girl of my dreams while sketching her picture. What could be more perfect than that?

Something causes that happiness to

quickly disappear though when I get into the downtown area. As I turn a corner and look down the street, I stop walking as I stare ahead of me in absolute horror. Alex is in front of my uncle's shop, casually leaning against the wall as if he is waiting for someone. I know who that someone is, me. Somehow, in the fraction of a second that I have to think, I toss all my art stuff behind a potted plant sitting in front of a women's clothing shop. As soon as I have that hidden, Alex spots me and a cold, cruel smile comes over his face as he starts walking toward me. I don't waste a second, I turn back the way I came and bolt down the street as fast as my legs can carry me.

I can barely hear anything over the sound of my blood pounding in my ears as I push myself to try and go faster. Even through the roar in my ears though, I can still hear Alex's footsteps getting closer and closer to me as he chases me down the street. I look all around me, trying to find someone who can help me, but there is nobody in sight. Why is the street so empty? Hope comes over me as I see an old man come out of a building and looks over to see me running away from Alex. He looks at the two of us for a second, seeing my panic, but he turns around and walks back inside the building, pretending that he didn't see anything. What? What just happened? Did that man really just leave me alone for Alex to do who knows what to me? What is wrong with him? I mean, I have had adults just walk away or ignore me when they have seen people picking on me, but how could he just leave me when Alex is clearly going to do something bad to me?! I can't let myself think about this though, I need to think of a way to get out of this and fast. I can practically hear Alex breathing behind me as he gets closer. I only have another minute or so before he is close enough to get me.

When I make it to the end of the strip of shops, I turn the corner, an idea suddenly coming into my head. If I can make it to the back door to my uncle's shop in the back alley, then I can get in and lock it behind me, so then Alex won't be able to get me. My lungs are burning from running so hard, but I force myself to go even faster. Everything is starting to ache as I can finally see the back door to my uncle's shop coming into view. I almost feel like laughing in joy when I am only a few feet away from the door, but that joy is suddenly killed.

I feel somebody grab me by the back of my shirt and, due to how fast I was running, my feet fly out from under me and I land on my back on the concrete road. I gasp for air since the wind got knocked out of me when I fell. I open my eyes to stare up at the blue sky. A dark chuckle comes from above me and the view of the beautiful sky is blocked out by Alex's face. He is smiling down at me with malicious glee, like an evil kid stepping on an ant hill.

"Oh poor Louie, you must have fallen down." I want to say something to him, tell him how much I hate him, but I am still gasping for air. Alex just smirks down at me, enjoying my pain. "Don't worry Louie, I'll help you out." He grabs me by the front of my shirt, and I try to pry his hands off of me, but it doesn't work. With his superior strength, he easily flips me over and shoves my face right into a puddle of water. One of his hands has a death grip on the hair on the back of my head, keeping me down in the water. I try to squirm out of his grip, to grab and swipe at his hand that is holding the back of my head, but it is no use. I try to move my head to get some air, but he holds me down, drowning me in that shallow puddle. Mud creeps into my nose and I can feel it getting splashed into my hair from how I am struggling to get out of Alex's grip. I can hear Alex chuckling above me as if this is some kind of game to him. He keeps me there long enough to make me think that he might kill me, then he appears to think that I have suffered enough. Keeping that same grip on my hair, he yanks my head back, out of the water. I take in several gasps of air, my lungs aching. He keeps his hand tangled in my hair as his voice comes from behind me, practically hissing in rage.

"Just because she's letting you do a picture of her doesn't mean anything. You are still the pathetic loser around here, and that will never change." He leans in closer so that he can whisper his final words right in my ear. "Face it Louie, you're nothing and you will die as nothing." With that said, he lets me go and he walks away as if nothing happened. As if this is something that he does all the time. I guess, in a way, he does do stuff like this all the time, mainly to me. I stay on the ground as I finally let my lungs have the air that they have wanted so desperately. I know that I should be terrified right now by what just happened, but as I lay on the ground, I find myself laughing. I laugh because I realize why Alex just did that. He is jealous and he wants to get back at me any way he can. He was wrong. I'm not the pathetic one. *He is.*

After I let myself have a good laugh, I pick myself up and walk right through the back door to my uncle's shop and head upstairs to the apartment we share. I take a few minutes cleaning the mud from that puddle off my face before I head back out to pick up the art stuff that I left behind. I make sure that Alex is nowhere to be seen before I leave the safety of my uncle's shop. When I see that the coast is clear, I make a run for the shop, quickly pick up my stuff, and then run back as if some of my demon shadow dogs are after me. Once I am in the safety of my room, I pass some time with Shadow. She was in a frenzy worrying about me over what just happened, but I just laughed it off until she finally got the picture that I didn't care. Now that night is here and I don't really have anything else to do, I look through some of the stuff I worked on today for the doctor's painting.

I glance over at the sketch I made with Colomba in the park on top of my dresser, propped up using an old sweater behind it. Earlier today, I was so happy when I called the doctor who ordered this painting since he told me that it would be perfectly alright to paint her again. He said that he just wanted a painting done by such a fantastic, young local artist. He didn't really care what the painting is of just as long as it looks good. I set up my easel and place a canvas on it while Shadow watches me with an amused look on her face.

"You always look so happy whenever you

are about to work on some of your art. It makes me happy to see so much joy within you." I smile back at her once I have my easel properly placed.

"Thanks, I do feel really good right now." Shadow nods her head at me, a thoughtful look coming over her feathered face.

"I'm guessing your happiness has more than just this painting as the cause. I'm guessing that you are also happy because of how Colomba has been treating Alex and how you believe he attacked you because he was jealous. Am I right?" I can't help but smile at her words.

"Yeah, that is true. It does feel nice that she isn't hanging around that creep anymore." She takes off into the air and perches on my shoulder so that she can look me directly in the eye.

"Are you sure that's your entire reason?" I stare into her eyes, trying to understand what she's really saying.

"What do you mean?" Shadow rolls her black eyes at me.

"I know how you felt when you saw how angry Alex was when he overheard Colomba saying that she would do the painting with you. You were happy that he felt miserable. Admit that." I lower my gaze, not wanting to look at her. I know that what she's saying makes me look very mean, but I also know it's true. I loved watching his pain, but he has always been so cruel to me, isn't that how I should feel? Shouldn't a person feel good when the person they hate is feeling miserable? I want to say that the answer is yes, but something in my heart says that the answer really is no. I should never be happy that somebody else is in pain. That would make me just as bad as Alex since he always enjoys making me feel pain.

"Okay, yeah I admit it. I did feel happy about that and I shouldn't have. Is that what you want to hear?" Shadow chuckles.

"Yes it is. Glad you're finally able to admit it. I was starting to think that I would never get it through that thick head of yours." I playfully glare at her as I shake her off my shoulder.

"Thanks, it's nice to know that I have you on my side." I mutter sarcastically as I start getting my paints ready to begin the painting. I start pulling out my tubes of paint and squeeze some of the paint onto a piece of cardboard so that I can dip my brush into it more easily. It almost feels like I'm gently squeezing a tube of toothpaste. I am starting to squeeze some paint on the board when Shadow speaks again.

"So when do you think that Alex will try and get back at you again?" In my surprise at her words, I squeeze the tube too hard and the paint splatters all over the cardboard. I clear my throat awkwardly and start dipping my brush in the paint as if nothing strange just happened. Oh my gosh, I should have thought of that. Alex is definitely going to try and get back at me because he's too angry to just let what happened in the alleyway a few hours ago be my only punishment. I am so doomed.

"I don't know, but knowing him, he will only do something when he has thought of the perfect revenge. He won't settle for anything else." Shadow nods at my words as I begin to spread paint along the canvas.

"Judging by how mad he looked, I'm going to guess that his plan will be very bad for you." I close my eyes and hold back a groan of misery. I know she's right, that's what is making me feel so much worse.

"Yeah, probably, but I'm not going to let that bother me. I can't control what he does, and besides I've already won. Colomba doesn't like him anymore and won't even speak to him. That's what he wants and he's not going to get it. There is no use in being upset since I have already won." Shadow nods her head.

"That is a very wise thing to believe. I would recommend that you watch your back though. When a person like that gets angry, you will never know what to expect." I look away from her so I can continue with my painting, but now my hands are clenched tightly around the brush in my anger.

"Don't worry, I already know that." Oh yes, I know just how much pain he can cause a person when he is upset.

One day, when we were in middle school, he was upset with me because I wouldn't let him copy off my test paper in English class. He didn't do anything to me that day, or even the day after that. I thought that he didn't care anymore, that he had forgotten about what I had done. I couldn't have been more wrong.

When I was heading out the front doors to head home after school he struck before I could even register what was happening. Several of his friends came out from behind the corner as I was walking toward the bus and dumped a few buckets full of paint on me that they had taken from the art room. I somehow was fast enough to close my eyes in time, but not fast enough to get out of the way.

After I had wiped the paint away from my closed eyes, I opened them to stare down at myself to see that I looked like a melting rainbow. Every color imaginable was spread all over me and was blending together as it dripped off of me and onto the ground in a very festive looking puddle. Alex and his little gang ran off before anybody could catch them, and nobody would have dared to tell the teachers who it was who did it. I tried to get on the bus to go home, but the bus driver wouldn't let me since he didn't want a huge mess all over his bus. I guess I can't blame him for that. When I tried to go into the school to tell them that I needed to borrow a phone so that I could call my uncle to take me home instead, they made me wait outside while they called him because they didn't want me to make a mess all over the floor. When I finally did get home about half an hour later, I had to spend around three hours just trying to get the paint off in the shower. I cried the entire time, continually calling myself a loser and spewing words of hate at Alex.

Yes, I know that I need to watch my back with him. I look down at my hand that's holding the paintbrush to see that my hand is shaking in fury at the memory. I take in a deep breath to calm myself as I continue to paint the peaceful scene in silence while chaos rages inside of me.

Chapter Seven
Colomba-
My Eager
Student

My face is lit up with a bright smile in my excitement as I wander through the halls as the final bell is ringing. Today is my first day in the tutoring program. I'm not old enough to have an actual job yet, so this is kind of my first job too. I make it to the classroom where this program is stationed to find several of the other students who have signed up to be tutors as well as several other students who will probably be the ones we are tutoring. The teacher in charge of this, Mrs. Caton, smiles at me as I come in.

"Hello Colomba, glad you're here, now we can get started assigning you all to who you will be tutoring." She goes through every person, assigning them to at least one other person. Once she has spoken to each person, they leave with the people they are tutoring to head into a different classroom to begin their lessons. She talks to everyone until I am the only one left with her in the room.

Confusion passes through me. Was nobody assigned to me? Did Mrs. Caton change her mind and decide that I shouldn't be a part of this program? I don't understand. Mrs. Caton smiles at me, probably trying to comfort me since she can see my confusion.

"The person you will be tutoring should be here any minute, he said that he would only be a few minutes late. He said that he just needed to speak to the coach first." She glances down at her shoes, as if she has suddenly become uncomfortable. "Colomba, I only want to start you out with one student first since this one will require some special attention. The coach for the football team wants us to pay particular attention to this student because if he doesn't get his grades up in math then he will be forced off the team. The coach is really relying on this student to help him win, especially this game coming up on Friday. The coach wants you to tutor him twice a week instead of the usual one day a week and you will be paid for the extra time. Do you think that you can take on the responsibility?" I nod my head at her.

"Of course, I will be happy to help anybody who needs me. Who is this person that I'll be tutoring?"

"Oh, his name is- Wait here he is." I turn around and my heart skips a beat, any trace of a smile is now gone from my face.

"Well hello there Beautiful." Alex smiles at me playfully, his eyes bright and eager. "I'm glad you'll be the one tutoring me. With you around this junk might actually be interesting." Mrs. Caton smiles at the two of us, not really noticing that I am no longer happy about this situation.

"Oh good, you two know each other already. I'm glad. That will make things easier for the both of you." Easier? No way is this going to be easier.

If I was somebody watching this, I would almost find this funny in an ironic way, but living through it is just painful. I want to refuse this position. I want to quit right now, but my dad and grandma didn't raise a quitter. I wanted to take this job. I was excited about it. I won't let someone like Alex ruin this opportunity for me. I'll just help him until his grades start going up, then I won't have to see him anymore. Just because I'm tutoring him doesn't mean that I have to hang out with him outside of here. He may try to get me to hang out with him again, but I don't have to say yes. I am in control here.

"Yes, we do know each other. C'mon Alex, let's go find another room where we can get started with the first lesson. Let's see how much you actually understand." My tone is cold, and I'm sure that he notices this, but it doesn't look like he cares. Alex simply follows after me with a smile on his face, as if he is completely confident that he can win me over and be friends with me again. Well he has another thing coming to him if he thinks that I will give in to him so easily. I won't let him win. I will never let him win after I saw the way he treated Luis. He will never win.

Chapter Eight
Luis-
Confusion

I walk through the halls to my third period, Advanced Art History, that I share with Colomba. I'm eager to talk to her about the progress I made on the painting last night. Using the sketches that we made the other day; I was able to do a good portion of the background but I would like to go with Colomba to the park someday soon so I can start painting her. Since she is the main part of the painting, I would like to actually see her while I am painting.

As I turn a corner, I see that Alex is leaning against a couple lockers right next to my classroom door. I know that he isn't looking for me though, he is waiting for Colomba. I put a smile on my face as I walk up to him. I was right when I spoke to Shadow the other night, I have no reason to be afraid of him. He may try to hurt me, but I have already won. I know this, and Alex knows it too. The pathetic part though is that he hasn't seemed to grasp that yet. Even though he knows that deep down, he hasn't let it sink in and he is still trying even though it is hopeless. Right now, he is wearing his football jersey, probably hoping that he can impress her with it, but she's not interested in stuff like that. She doesn't really care about sports, unless the sport is martial arts and swordsmanship, she's awesome at those sports. Alex notices my smiling face as I walk closer to the classroom door.

"What are you so happy about, freak?" I grin at him, as if I have no hatred for him.

"Oh I guess I'm just happy because I got to paint Colomba the other day and I'm getting paid a ton of money to do it and I get to hang out with her. Who wouldn't be happy with a deal like that?" Alex glares at me for a moment, thinking of a cruel comeback. It doesn't take very long before a cold smile crawls across his face.

"Yeah, but I don't think that will last very long. The two of us are getting friendly again and we even got to hang out after school yesterday. I doubt she would want to hang out with you if she could be hanging out with me." My heart stops as I listen to his words. Is what he is saying true? Did Colomba hang out with him yesterday? Are they starting to become friends again? My thoughts race for only a moment before I realize the obvious. He is just messing with me. Nothing he said is true. He just wants me to worry about nothing, well it's not going to work.

What helps me prove that point in my mind is that Colomba is walking toward the two of us now. She is smiling warmly at me, but not even looking at Alex. Something that makes me feel even better is that she is wearing the necklace that I got for her when we were at the county fair over the summer.

"Hi Luis, how are you?" My smile grows wider as she completely ignores Alex beside me.

"I'm doing great, how are you?" The two of us start walking slowly to the classroom door, leaving Alex behind us.

"I'm doing great, how is the painting coming along?"

"It's doing great." I make sure to ask her a question while I still have Alex within earshot. "Hey, do you think that you could model for me again on Friday afternoon? I would really like to finish it up as soon as possible and I think that it would help a lot if we went back to the same place we started." Colomba nods her head at me.

"Of course, I would be happy to help." Colomba walks into the room while I stay behind for a moment to give Alex a quick, evil smirk of triumph. What surprises me though is that the look of surprise on his face is there for only a second before it is replaced by a smile even darker than mine. He flashes that smile at me before walking away with his head held high. I watch after him, curious as to why he looked that way. Does he have something planned? I don't have time to think about that though. As I watch him the class bell rings, and I rush inside the room so that I can get to my seat so class can begin.

Chapter Nine
Colomba-
Tutoring Alex

"Okay, so to solve for the hypotenuse, or the longest side of the triangle, you must use the equation A squared plus B squared equals C squared. C squared is the hypotenuse while the other two numbers are the other sides of the triangle. Do you get that?" Alex and I are sitting at a table in a classroom by ourselves for tutoring. Even though I am drawing the triangle out on the paper in front of us to explain it to him, he isn't even looking at it. He is only looking at me, just like he has been doing every second since we got in here. I sigh softly, feeling irritated.

"Alex, have you been paying attention to anything I've said? You got into this tutoring program so that you can stay on the football team. Judging on how much you love playing football, I would have guessed that you would try to put in a bit more effort." Alex chuckles as he stretches his arms above his head, probably trying to show off his muscles underneath his football jersey. He has been wearing that thing almost every day this week.

Has he at least been washing it? If not, that's super gross.

"Of course, I'm paying attention to you. I can't take my eyes off of you." It takes every ounce of self-control in my body not to roll my eyes at that pathetic excuse of flirting.

"I've noticed." I mutter sarcastically. "What I really want you to look at though is this triangle so that you can learn how to find the hypotenuse." Alex chuckles again, as if I am joking.

"Maybe I could concentrate better on this if we could meet in a more relaxed place. Maybe if I took you out to dinner, that might be a lot more relaxing. Maybe I could take you out after the game on Friday. I know I will win if I have you watching me from the stands." This time, I do roll my eyes.

"No thanks Alex, I don't want to go, and I don't even like football. I also already have plans. Can we please just get on with this so we can go home?" My harsh words can't even make a dent in that confident grin of his.

"Oh, I forgot to mention something." I close my eyes, getting ready for him to give me another stupid pickup line. "I will need to have an extra day of tutoring this week because I have a huge math test next week. Would Friday after school work for you?" I look up from my paper to stare at him with curiosity.

"Didn't you hear me say just a second ago that I already have plans on Friday? Also, don't you have a football game that night? Wouldn't you be preparing after school?" Alex chuckles at me.

"I have some time right after school to do

the tutoring. I'm sure that you can change your plans to fit this in." Oh my gosh, this guy actually wants me to change my plans just to meet his needs? What a selfish jerk!

"Alex I can't do that. Luis is relying on me to help him with a painting he's working on and I can't let him down."

"Oh c'mon Colomba, you can do that any day. Besides, if I don't pass my math class then I will get kicked off the team and we have plenty of games after this that I need to play in. You don't want to let the school down, do you?" My mouth suddenly grows dry and I have no idea what I am going to do. I don't really care about football, or really any sports at all besides martial arts and swordsmanship, but I know that everybody else in this school really cares a lot about the sports teams, especially the football team. Alex has always showed off to me about how he is the star player on the team, and he is right. If he gets kicked off the team because he can't improve his grades, then the team will probably lose a lot of games. If that happens then everyone will be upset, and I don't want that. I also don't want to let Luis down by having to reschedule our painting session. He is one of my best friends, and he looked so excited when I said that I would do it for him. I would hate to see him disappointed.

I am tempted to tell Alex that I can't do it, but then I remember how excited everyone gets whenever Alex or one of the other team members walks down the hall in their jersey near game day. I don't want to see that excitement fade from my school. I release a small sigh as I turn back to face Alex.

"Alright, I can reschedule it, but you need to promise me that you will pay attention then. If this test is that big then we have a lot of catching up to do." The two of us get back to work while a dark cloud seems to hang over me.

Chapter Ten
Luis-
One Plan Canceled,
A New One Comes

Today is Friday and everyone is buzzing with excitement for the big football game tonight. Practically everyone is wearing the school colors of red and black and talking about how much they hope that our team will win. I've also heard a few people say that with Alex on the team, there is no way that we can lose. I don't have to worry about this though because I don't care about sports, and I also have other plans. Today is the day that I take Colomba to the park to do some more work on the painting. I have been looking forward to this ever since we made the plan the other day. Right now, I am heading toward my third period class. I'm in a bit of a hurry today since I am running late. I make it inside the classroom just in time as the bell is ringing to start the class.

I sit down in my seat beside Colomba, giving her a quick smile before I give my full attention to Mr. Sizemore as he starts teaching us about the Impressionist art movement. Class moves by quickly for me and it only feels as if a couple minutes have passed before the bell rings again to signal the end of class. Standing, I pick up my stuff in one movement and turn to Colomba with a broad smile.

"Hello Colomba, it's great to see you." She smiles back at me, but it seems a bit halfhearted, as if she is just smiling to be polite but isn't actually happy. The two of us walk out of the classroom together and into the hallway.

"Hey Luis, what's up? I tried calling you a few times yesterday and you didn't answer." I feel suddenly happy, knowing that she tried so hard to call me.

"I'm sorry but I dropped my phone in a puddle yesterday, so it spent the rest of the night in a bag of rice. Is something wrong?" She lowers her head, showing some guilt. What on earth could she ever feel bad about? I don't think I have ever heard her say a mean word to anyone, let alone do anything bad.

"Yes, there is something wrong. I'm sorry Luis, but I can't make it to our painting session today. I have to meet up with Alex later. I've got to get going to my next class. Have a good day." I stare after her, every sound in the hallway seems to disappear except for the pounding of my heart as she leaves. She has to "meet up with Alex"? What does that mean? Is she friends with him again or is it something worse? *Are they going on a date?*

I try to take in a breath of air, but it feels as if I'm not breathing in anything. It's almost as if all the air in the hallway has disappeared. I turn around when I hear a familiar chuckle coming from behind me. Alex is leaning against the lockers, smiling wickedly. He saw what just happened and he looks as if he has found paradise. He is happy that I am so miserable.

"Too bad Louie, did your little drawing play date get canceled?" His voice sounds like someone teasing a child. I want to punch him right through his smiling teeth, but he would probably do a lot worse to me if I did that, so I keep my hands at my sides, clenched into fists and shaking with rage. Something in the back of my mind tells me that Alex planned all this. He heard me making plans with Colomba to paint today and so he somehow convinced her to make plans with him and break off her plans with me. Alex laughs again when he glances down to see my fists quivering with rage.

"Don't be so upset Louie, you should have expected this. I mean, why would she want to hang out with a pathetic little boy like you when she could spend her time with a *man* like me? It's only natural for her to prefer me over you. Just get used to it Louie, that's the way it's going to be and there's nothing you can do to change it." He shakes his head as he smiles cruelly. "I almost feel sorry for you." I doubt you have ever felt sorry for anyone in your life, you monster. "I feel sorry that such a worthless creep like you actually exists and has to compete in life with someone like me. The world is just setting you up for failure. Might as well face it Louie, you're never going to get anything good in your life when someone like me is competing with you, especially if we both want a girl as pretty as Colomba. Maybe you should go out and try to find someone else, you know, someone with really low standards. Then things might actually work out for you and you could get a girlfriend. You just need to find someone as pathetic as you." He gives me one last cold chuckle as he takes in one last glance at my defeated figure before he turns away and leaves me alone to stare after him.

My stomach feels as it is slowly crushing itself, I think I might throw up. My throat tightens as I feel my eyes beginning to grow warm, and I know that I'm about to cry. I blink my eyes hard as I try to force the tears away. No, I will not let this happen. I won't let him get close to her again. He will bring her nothing but pain.

I march down the hall and head to my next class. My hands are gripped so tightly around my books that my knuckles are turning white. When I get into my classroom, I sit down in my chair and stare ahead at the whiteboard at the front of the room until the bell rings. I wait for a few minutes before I ask the teacher if I can go to the bathroom.

My footsteps echo on the tile floor of the hallway while my heart pounds in my rage. I push the door to the bathroom wide open and sweep my eyes across the room to see that nobody else is there. When I see that I am alone, I place my hand on top of my Crow Medal. Shadow appears on top of the paper towel dispenser, but I am too furious to even bother saying hello to her.

"Shadow, transform me into the Crow. It's

time we showed the world the kind of monster that Alex is." Shadow looks at me for a moment, worry clouding her black eyes before she takes off into the air and flies around me so quickly that all I can see is a circle of blackness around me. I close my eyes for only a second, and when I open them again I have become the Crow. Usually, I feel a lot better when I have transformed myself. I feel stronger and I don't have any fear like I do when I walk around this school as my usual self. Today is different though. Today I have hatred controlling me, and I can't feel any kind of happiness.

"Shadow, find Alex." I can sense Shadow's confusion as she flies out of the bathroom and into the hallway. She flies as a shadow on the wall, practically invisible except to those who pay close attention to the world around them. It doesn't take long for Shadow to find my prey.

Alex is walking down the hall with his head held high, wearing his football jersey with the pride of a king wearing a crown. He probably also feels proud since he knows that he has stolen Colomba from me, but that won't last. Since he is alone in the hall, I make my move. Shadow flies straight into his cold, cruel heart and I make myself known to him.

Hello Alex. Alex turns around quickly, his hands raised into fists. I smile to myself when I feel his confusion and fear. His heart beats faster in his chest when he realizes that he is completely alone in this hallway.

I am the Crow Alex, and I am here to

help you. Alex clears his throat and lets his body return to its usual proud posture.

"Why do you want to help me? What can you do for me?" In Alex's mind, he is excited as he thinks about how I'm probably going to give him superpowers. He's hoping that he can use those powers to get everything he wants. He imagines himself taking control of this school (at least more control than he has already) and making everyone in it do whatever he wants. Jeez this guy is a psycho. I'm the one everyone says is a villain in this school, but this guy is the one scaring me.

Let's just say that I have been watching you closely and I know that you are anxious to win the game that is happening tonight. I can give you the strength so that you can take down any enemy. You will be stronger than anyone else. I'm sure that's something you want. What do you say?

Alex stays silent for a moment, pretending to think it over, but I know how he really feels. In his mind he is practically bursting with excitement. He is eager to use the power I am about to give him to finally get everything he wants; power, respect, and everyone to be a bit afraid of him.

"Alright, make me strong Crow. I'm ready to take on the world." I chuckle to myself. He probably means that he's ready to take over the world, but I don't bother to correct him.

With pleasure. Shadow lets herself invade the rest of him, slowly taking over every part of his body. Alex's eyes open wide in terror as he lets out a moan of agony. With everyone else I transformed I made the transformation painless, but not for him. I let Alex feel his skin stretch as his bones grow within him. He holds back screams in his pain, only releasing moans and growls in his torture. The transformation only lasts for a minute, and the final touch that I add is something that makes Alex lose his strong composure as I let two horns rip out of the top of his head. He doesn't scream when this happens, like what a normal person would do. No, what Alex releases is a roar. When the transformation is over, he stands on his hands and knees, breathing heavily. He no longer sounds human, even his thoughts aren't normal.

Oh yes, he is strong now alright. I didn't tell him something kind of important though. I transformed him so that he would be incredibly strong, but now he is also dumb as a rock and will follow any command I give him. Let the fun begin.

Chapter Eleven
Colomba-
The Monster

My hand races across the page as I start to work on a few math problems that the teacher is having us do. I am in my Advanced Placement Algebra class right now, a class I usually like, but today is different. Today my heart is filled with misery because I know that I have disappointed my friend. The look on Luis' face when I told him that I couldn't meet up with him today almost killed me. His smile immediately disappeared, and his eyes just looked at me with pain, especially when I said that I had to meet up with Alex instead of meeting with him. I know that Luis really doesn't like Alex, it must have hurt him so much to think that I was choosing Alex over him. I didn't do that though. I did it because of what Alex said. I don't want to let the school down. I don't want him to get kicked off the team and have the team fail because of that. I just hope that I can explain it to Luis sometime later today. I couldn't explain it to him then because I couldn't stand seeing the pain on his face a second longer. Isn't that understandable?

Even though it is calm in the room, my eyes open wide in fear and my chest tightens in terror. I know what this feeling is. It is one of the powers I have with my Dove Pin, the ability to sense when something bad is about to happen. I silently glance around the room, trying to find anything unusual, but everyone is just working on the equations as if everything is perfectly normal. When I suddenly realize where I sense the danger is coming from, it is too late.

The door seems to explode from a massive force coming inside from the hallway. Everyone either leaps up or falls out of their chairs in surprise. A terrible grunting sound, like the sounds that come from a huge animal are coming from outside the door. Everyone in the classroom remains in silence as we watch something come into the room with footsteps that pound on the floor like a hammer.

My heart stops in my chest at the terrible sight that comes through the doorway. A massive creature, more hideous than anything I have ever seen is standing right in front of me. The creature has the body of a man, but completely covered in grey fur. What truly terrifies me though is the head of this creature. The head isn't human like the body, instead it looks like the head of a massive bull. Two pointed, menacing horns stick out of the creature's head while two horrific glowing red eyes glare at everyone in the classroom. The creature releases grunting noises as it breathes, and it swings its extremely muscled arms as it walks further into the room. Something about the creature makes the hairs on the back of my neck stand up straight in horror. It is wearing a football jersey. Not just any jersey though. This is the jersey that all the football players in my school wear. My horror only grows when I recognize the number thirteen on the jersey. That's Alex's number, that's his jersey number. This creature is Alex.

Wait, how can this creature be Alex? This is definitely the work of the Crow and the Crow only transforms people who are being bullied. People say that Alex is the bully though, why has the Crow transformed him? This doesn't make any sense. I don't have time to stop and think about this though. The creature lunges toward me faster than I would have thought possible with his massive bulk. One hand grabs me by my dress and lifts me high into the air. The creature lets out a roar of triumph and then pauses for a moment, as if it is listening to someone. I have a feeling that the Crow is the one whispering in its head, and I am not eager to find out what the Crow is telling this beast to do with me. Before I can even think of a way to escape, I am saved by someone I would never have expected.

Luis runs into the room through the broken door and straight toward the creature, holding a small potted plant that the teacher was using as a decoration on her desk. Without any fear whatsoever, Luis throws the plant at the creature's head. It makes a satisfying crashing sound when it hits it and shatters into a million pieces on the floor. The creatures lets out a roar of pain as he drops me to the ground. I land in a crumpled heap on the floor, a surge of pain ignites in my ankle as I do so, but I don't stay there very long. Luis quickly picks me up in his arms and rushes out the door with me along with the rest of the class and my teacher. The class scatters in the hallway to find someplace to hide. Apparently, the rest of the school is probably hiding right now too since everything is silent and nobody else is in sight. Luis doesn't stop running though until he has gotten us both safely hidden in a janitor's closet. The two of us sit on the ground, the room around us reeking of cleaning chemicals. He still holds me in his arms, as if he is afraid that I will run back to that creature again or something.

"Are you alright Colomba?" he whispers, probably trying not to make any loud noises so that monster won't come near us. I nod my head.

"Yeah, yeah I'm alright. My ankle hurts though from when he dropped me." I whisper back to him. Luis looks down at my ankle, his gaze clouded with worry. He bends down to examine it.

"Don't be afraid, I've taken some classes on basic first aid. I just want to check and see if you are hurt." I feel my eyes narrow slightly in suspicion as he examines my ankle. Where have I heard that before? I could swear that I have heard someone tell me that before when my ankle was injured, but I don't think it was a good memory. Was I afraid when it happened before? Who else has said that to me? And why do I suddenly feel nervous?

"I don't think it's anything to worry about." Luis says with a relieved smile. "I think it just got sprained a little. You'll be fine if you just relax and not stand on it for a little bit."

"Thank goodness." Even though my words show relief, worry bounces through my brain. I can't transform into Silver Dove to stop this thing if Luis is with me and Luis won't leave me since I am injured. It appears that I am going to be stuck in this position for a while considering I can't just run away from Luis to transform because of my ankle. I might as well try to act the part so he doesn't become suspicious. I need to act how any other person would in this situation, I act afraid.

"Luis what are we supposed to do? This is so scary. I don't know what to do." He gives me a gentle hug to try and comfort me.

"Don't worry. Everything will be alright. As soon as this thing has finished what it started it will go away, or Silver Dove will beat it up or something. Either way, all we have to do is wait." We sit in silence for a moment before I speak again.

"That thing, that was Alex. It had his number on its jersey. Why would the Crow want to change Alex? He usually transforms bullied kids, not the bully. This doesn't make any sense." Luis nods his head as he thinks of what to say.

"Maybe he just wants the world to see Alex the way he does; a big stupid monster." I don't say anything in response to that. What can be said to that? I guess that is what most people view Alex as, and I don't think they would be wrong. I mean Alex isn't the sharpest knife in the drawer, I will admit that. I have seen a lot of evidence for that during our tutoring sessions, and from what I have heard, he is constantly hurting others. I guess that he would be seen as a monster to other people. I try not to see people in that way, but right now I can't help but agree. Maybe Alex really is a monster.

The two of us hold on to each other and I make myself shiver a little to make me appear a bit more afraid to Luis. I need to make this look good or Luis will be confused as to why I'm not terrified of a creepy monster that could have killed me only a few moments ago. As we hold each other in the silence, I try to think of a way to solve this mess. A thousand thoughts swirl in my brain, but none of them are a solution.

Chapter Twelve
Luis-
Controlling My
Monster

I hold Colomba close as we both silently sit in the janitor's closet. This didn't go exactly as planned, and I don't think I'm really liking how it is turning out. I wanted him to come in and scare everyone, but especially Colomba. I did all this so that she can see him the way I do, the way everyone in this school does, a monster. I told him to grab her, to help scare her and make me look a bit like a hero, but I didn't expect her to hurt her ankle when he dropped her. I feel really bad about that. I never want her to ever get hurt. I would rather go through every pain imaginable than let her get hurt.

She is in my arms now as we both sit here in this smelly closet. She is shivering so badly in her terror that my guilt builds every second and I feel as if I may just snap. I don't want her to be afraid anymore, I think that she has learned the lesson I was trying to teach her. She sees Alex as he really is, the monster in this school. Now that she knows this, it is time for this to end. At least for now.

I let my mind travel through the school until I find the creature. He is rampaging through the gym right now, tearing apart the bleachers with his horns.

Alex! The creature stops what it is doing to stupidly stare around the room, expecting to find me there even though I have spoken in its head many times before. I'm not there you stupid cow! I am in your head! We have been through this about ten times already! You need to leave the school now and head into the woods right outside of town until I need you again!

"I… go… woods?!" The creature yells to the empty room. I have to hold back a sigh at him. Why did I make him this stupid? I know I had to make him stupid so that he would follow every order I give him, but did he really need to be this stupid? It's kind of getting frustrating now. It was pretty funny at first, but now I'm just irritated.

Yes! Yes, you idiot! That's what I just said! Now go before I get angry and turn you into something even more terrible than this!

The creature doesn't need me to say anymore. It rushes out of the room and down the hall, running on all fours so that it can move faster. Whenever something stands in its way in the hall, it bashes it aside using its horns without stopping. The creature runs right past the janitor's closet that Colomba and I are hiding in, creating a roar of noise from its thundering footsteps. Colomba jumps a little in surprise, which makes her whimper a little when she moves her hurt ankle. I hold her closer as a wave of guilt comes over me. She shouldn't have gotten hurt. I shouldn't have let that happen. I listen as the creature crashes through the doors leading outside and runs across the school parking lot. After a few minutes, everything is silent.

"Did he leave?" Colomba asks in complete disbelief.

"I guess so." Colomba slowly crawls toward the door and opens it a crack, glancing out to see that the entire hallway is clear and a huge hole where the doors leading outside used to be before that creature ran straight through them.

"Why did he leave? I don't think anything really happened, he just left." I shrug my shoulders.

"I don't know. Maybe the Crow wants him to do something else." Her eyes grow wide in horror.

"You don't think he will have that thing attack the town, do you?" I shake my head at her.

"No, I don't think so. This school is the Crow's battleground, he won't do anything to the town." She looks at me with confusion.

"Battleground? You make him sound like a soldier fighting a war." The two of us stare at each other in silence for a moment before I say what I feel needs to be said.

"Maybe he is." She stares at me for a moment in disbelief before she looks away with a thoughtful expression. Wow, I may have had two victories today. I have helped her see the way everyone sees Alex, and I may have made her feel some sympathy for the Crow even though she has openly admitted to hating me. "I think we should stay in here just a few minutes more just to make sure that he's gone." Colomba nods at me.

"Yeah, that makes sense. That's a good idea." She leans against the wall as she stares at nothing. She is obviously thinking about something, I can only hope that she's thinking about how her opinions have changed about me.

Chapter Thirteen
Colomba-
Whispers In
The Hall

All is silent as Luis and I wait for something to happen, but it feels as if the entire world has stopped moving. It is that quiet. I look up at Luis, who is still holding me close while his ear is pressed up against the door so that he can hear what is happening on the other side.

"Do you hear anything?" I whisper to him. He pauses for a moment as he listens to the silence in the hall behind the door.

"I think that it's gone. Whatever it was." I release a sigh. I want it to sound like I am relieved since I want Luis to think that I am still scared by all of this. I'm actually a bit mad that the creature is gone. I was hoping that Luis would leave me for a moment, or that my ankle would feel better so that I could run away and transform into Silver Dove and get rid of that thing. Why did it leave anyway? This isn't really the Crow's style. He usually keeps attacking until I have to step in to stop him. What is he planning? Is he just going to make that thing stay quiet for a little while and just pop out again at a random time so that I won't expect it?

As Luis and I leave the janitor's closet, he keeps his arm around me so that I can lean against him while I limp on my hurt ankle. It does feel a lot better than it did before, but it still stings whenever I try to walk on it. The two of us jump as a voice comes over the intercom and breaks the silence.

"Good afternoon students." The voice of the principal calls out in a bit of a frightened voice. "It appears that the danger has now passed, our procedure against the Crow's attack seems to have worked perfectly since nobody seems to have been hurt." Nobody was hurt? Really? I guess he's not including me with my throbbing ankle. "Since Silver Dove was not able to appear and fix everything like usual," I hear a note of anger in his voice, as if that is my job and I have disappointed him, what a jerk, "and we cannot let our students continue to go to class in a broken school, so you are all allowed to go home early today. The game later tonight will still take place though since the football field seems to have not been damaged. The buses have been notified and will be arriving in a few minutes to bring everyone home. Have a good evening students, and make sure to come and cheer on the Drew's Hollow Horsemen tonight." It doesn't take long for countless students to pour out of the classrooms and down the hall to head out the front doors. As Luis helps me along, I look at all the damage that creature did.

Lockers are torn apart and ripped off the walls

while some of the walls have massive holes in them. I look away from them, suddenly feeling guilty.

I should have found a way to get away from Luis so that I could transform. I should have stopped all this destruction. It doesn't really help me feel any better when two girls pass by us and I overhear their conversation.

"I can't believe nothing happened. Why didn't Silver Dove stop that disgusting thing? Where was she anyway?" The friend they're talking to just shrugs.

"I don't know, maybe Silver Dove just doesn't care anymore. Maybe she's just tired of saving the day and wants us to solve our problems by ourselves. I would do that. I wouldn't want to solve everyone else's problems all the time. I've got better things to do." The girl who spoke first just shakes their head at their friend.

"Well then what are we supposed to do, just wait until that thing comes back and kills us all?" Now it is the friend's turn to shake their head.

"Nope, I'm sure that somebody will figure something out since Silver Dove is too lazy to save us this time." The two of them walk past us while my heart sinks into my chest. Does everyone think of me that way? After everything I have done for them, they think that I am abandoning them so that they can fall under the mercy of the Crow? How could they do that to me? As these thoughts swirl in my brain, another thought thankfully comes in to take their place. Alex. He was definitely that creature. The problem is knowing where and when he will be coming back. Knowing the Crow, he will probably make it come back at a super dramatic moment. This guy does seem to enjoy being dramatic. If he is going to be dramatic like he usually is, then the best place to have that thing come back would be at the football game tonight. The principal did say that the game will still happen. I turn to Luis to see what he thinks.

"Do you think that the Crow will make that thing come back at the football game tonight?" Luis looks thoughtful for a moment before a light seems to spark in his eyes, as if he has suddenly realized something.

"That would be the perfect time for it to come back, wouldn't it?" Do I hear excitement in his voice?

"Yeah, I'm going to go tonight to see what happens. Do you want to come with me?" his already big smile somehow is able to get bigger.

"Sure, that sounds great." The two of us fall silent again as my mind goes through everything that just happened, and a single question pops into my mind that makes my stomach twist into knots. How did Luis know that I was in trouble with that creature so that he could come in and rescue me? He wasn't even in that class with me, so how did he know? I glance up at him, suddenly nervous.

"Hey Luis, how did you know that I was in trouble with that thing? You weren't even in that class with me, so how did you know to come and find me?" His eyes grow wide with surprise for only a moment, so quickly that I almost didn't notice it. That disappears though and he smiles down at me with amusement.

"I was just walking down the hall to go to the library when I saw that thing go into the classroom, and I knew you were in there, so I ran over just in time." He continues to smile down at me, as if anxiously waiting for my reply. Something about what he just said doesn't seem right. It almost feels as if Luis is lying to me, but I can't let my mind be filled with that right now. I have more important things to think about, like how am I going to find and defeat that creature?

"Thank you for that Luis, I really am grateful that you did that for me." He nods as he beams at me with his usual friendliness, his nervousness gone.

"Not a problem." The two of us continue walking to our bus in silence. My mind is filled with so many things, but I don't know what to do. As Luis helps me hobble through the halls on my hurt ankle, I try not to listen to the people around me who all seem to be asking the same question. Where was Silver Dove?

Chapter Fourteen
Luis-
Before The
Game

I pull a jacket out of my closet as I watch the sun beginning to set outside the window of my room. My uncle will be taking me to the game in a couple minutes. He seemed very surprised that I wanted to go since I have told him countless times how much I hate sports. Truthfully, I've never really paid attention to sports, the reason I say that I hate them is because most of my worst bullies are on the school sports teams. It's hard to like something if all the people you hate are the ones doing it. I slip the jacket on while Shadow is perched on top of my windowsill.

"You seem very excited Master." She states with that dark tone which warns me that she is about to scold me as if she is my mom.

"I am. I get to show the entire town what Alex really is at the game tonight. Colomba was right, this will be the perfect place for him to pop back up in. Everyone has always thought that he is the best, I want to show them that he really is the worst. That he is the one who deserves to be hurt, not all the people he picks on every day. This is something that I have always wanted to do." Shadow flies off the windowsill and onto my dresser so that she can be closer to me.

"But I do not believe that this is what you intended to use your powers for. Didn't you say that it was part of your mission to give powers to other bullied kids so that they could get revenge and scare everyone into treating each other better? How does this help with your mission?" I turn away from her, not wanting to look into her dark, questioning eyes.

"Well, maybe I need to change my tactics a bit. What I've been doing up to now hasn't worked so I should try something different." I hear Shadow chuckle behind me.

"'Change my tactics'? Colomba was right, you really do sound like a soldier fighting a war." She sighs softly before she speaks again. "You know that I will follow you, whatever choice you make, but I just want to make sure that you are making the right decisions so that you can succeed in your mission. I don't want you to work so hard just to fail because you became upset." I glare at her.

"I didn't do this because I was upset, I did this because it needs to be done." Shadow shakes her head at me as if I am acting silly.

"Master, you know that I can read you whenever I am in the medal you are wearing, I know what you were thinking. You were angry because Colomba said that she had to be with Alex instead of working on the painting with you and you wanted to get back at Alex." I let go of some of my anger when I realize that she is right and there is no point in arguing against her, she really does know exactly what I was thinking.

"Alright fine, yes I was upset, but he still deserves this. He has always been cruel to me and he knew that Colomba was going to be with me, but he got her to go on a date with him at the exact same time."

"I don't think that it was supposed to be a date." Shadow says a bit uncomfortably. "Colomba never said that it was, you just assumed that. They could have been meeting up for many reasons, but I doubt that it was supposed to be a date." I feel the rage rise in me again.

"Of course it was supposed to be a date. Why else would they be meeting up? Why else would she decide to break her plans with me to be with him? He just wants to make me suffer. Why does he love to hurt me the most?"

"I believe that the real question you should be asking yourself is why is he so cruel to begin with." I look at her, all my rage completely forgotten, as I stare at her in confusion.

"What are you talking about Shadow?" She flies onto my shoulder and stares into my eyes.

"No matter what somebody does, there is always a reason why. Perhaps there is a reason why Alex treats you like he does. Maybe there is something in his life that none of us knows about." I roll my eyes as I shrug her off my shoulder. She flies off and lands on my dresser again.

"I don't care what his reasons are! He is a terrible person! No matter what happens to you, you shouldn't take it out on other people."

"C'mon Tigre, we need to go! We don't want to be late!" I hear my uncle call out from the living room. I look to Shadow, releasing all of my anger, reminding myself that for the first time in my life I have Alex under my control.

"Things will go well tonight Shadow. I will finally stand up to Alex and be victorious over him." Shadow nods solemnly.

"I hope that you get what you need tonight Master." She states this before she flies off the dresser and into the medal, disappearing inside it. I cover the medal with my jacket and head out of my room to meet up with my uncle so that he can take me to the game. I take in a deep breath to try and calm myself. There is a lot that I plan will happen tonight, and I must remain calm. If I am calm, then I will be able to focus and crush anyone who stands in my way, maybe even Silver Dove.

Chapter Fifteen
Colomba-
Riding To
The Game

My grandmother's car slowly glides down the country road heading into town. The sun is just beginning to set, making the world around us look a little creepy in the fading light. With the limited light, the trees almost seem to close in around us, like monsters getting ready to pounce on our little car. My stomach feels as if it is doing backflips inside of me. I am so nervous about what is going to happen. Will Alex show up as that creepy monster again, or will he be back to normal? If he does come back as that monster, can I still defeat him? That thing looked bigger and nastier than anything I have ever faced before. With everything that the Crow has been attacking me with, that's really saying something. My grandma seems to have noticed how badly I feel since her sweet, gentle voice invades my negative thoughts.

"What is bothering you Tesoro?" I turn

away from the window to look at her. I told her and my dad about what happened at school today, but she didn't seem that worried about it. She seemed more curious when I mentioned that Alex was the one who got transformed, that really got her attention.

"I'm just worried about what's going to happen at the game tonight." She nods her head in understanding.

"It is a painful thing to not know what to expect. I'm sure that you will do well though. You have fought the Crow many times now and you have always won. You will win again." I feel a little better when I hear how confident she sounds. I wish I could be that confident with myself right now. One thought still nags me in the back of my mind though. It's been in my mind almost all day, but now I finally say it out loud to her.

"Why do you think the Crow transformed Alex? He only changes bullied kids, but Alex is the bully." My grandmother stares ahead at the road in front of us, a thoughtful look on her face.

"Do you think, perhaps, that he is trying to make a point?"

"What do you mean?" She goes silent for a moment, as if trying to figure out how to explain herself.

"He said that his mission is to get rid of all the bullies. After everything he has done, everyone still treats Alex as if he is a hero whenever a game is coming up. Maybe he wants everyone to look at Alex the way he sees him. You said that this creature he turned Alex into is an overly muscled, stupid brute. Maybe that's how he views Alex." I stare out the window as I think about what she said.

I think I can understand why he would view Alex like that. He is a bit of a pain in the neck at the best of times, I can only imagine how unbearable he would be if I was one of the people he was bullying. Alex isn't a smart guy, I know that from the few days I've been tutoring him, and he can act like a complete jerk even when he's not trying to be. Maybe the Crow is showing Alex in his true light. I don't really know what to think right now. Should I feel bad for the Crow, or Alex, or neither of them? I only know that I need to stop all this no matter who is right or not because I don't want anybody to get hurt.

"If he starts transforming all the bullies in this school, then nobody will be safe from him and we will all live in fear."

"I don't think that is true. The Crow would not do something like that." I turn away from the window to look at her with surprise.

"What are you talking about? This guy is completely crazy, how can you defend him?" She falls silent again while I stare at her, waiting impatiently for her answer.

"I view this boy, the Crow, as someone who has been hurt far too many times and doesn't know how to make things better so he is just doing anything he can to try. He wants things to get better, not just for himself but for all the other kids like him. Maybe you shouldn't think and talk about him as if he is your enemy, maybe you should view him the way you look at everyone else in your school.

View him as someone you need to help save." She smiles softly as the sun finally sets on the horizon and the world is plunged into darkness. "The Crow does have a good heart. He has a good heart but a broken soul."

I feel the car stop and I look out the window to see that we have already arrived at the school's football field. A large line is already formed in front of the ticket booth and I can see Luis standing off to the side waiting for me. I turn back to face my grandmother.

"Are you sure that you don't want to come to the game with us?" She smiles at me with amusement.

"If there is going to be a battle like you think there will be, that would not be the place for an old woman like me." I smile too when I realize how ridiculous it was for me to ask that. "Don't worry, you will do fine. You will defeat him like the little warrior you are." She gives me a quick kiss goodbye before I step out of the car to join Luis, my heart pounding harder than a drum in my nervousness. I can only hope that my grandmother is right and that I will be fine.

Chapter Sixteen
Luis-
The Big
Game

Everyone is crowded close together as we all make our way through the entry way and to the stands where I can tell that over a hundred people are already sitting. The game won't start for another half hour, yet I can tell that it's going to be packed. Everyone looks very upset as they chat with each other. They think that without Alex our team doesn't stand a chance. They are also afraid that they will never see Alex again, that he is now under the complete control of the Crow. I smile when I hear them say that, I will soon show them just how right they are.

Colomba is walking beside me. My smile grows even bigger when I see that she is walking just fine on the ankle she had hurt earlier today with my creature. I still feel a bit guilty whenever I think about that. Tonight though, I will make sure that she doesn't get hurt. I will stay by her side to make sure that nothing happens when I bring my creature back. He is currently waiting for my order in a clump of trees half a mile away. I can feel the excitement going through his tiny mind as he waits. He is eager to get over here and cause some damage. I can only hope that he can do some damage to Silver Dove if she shows up.

That is something that everyone is talking about too, where was Silver Dove earlier today when my creature first attacked the school? Was she sick or something so she was absent from school? Or did something get in her way? My mind rushes through countless possible answers to that question, but I know that I will never find the answer, so I just decide to enjoy the moment.

Colomba is looking around the crowd with delight. She told me a bit earlier that this is the first football game she has ever been to. I am sad to say that this is my second. The first one didn't go very well.

I was in elementary school and my uncle decided to take me to one of the games, probably since he thought it was pathetic that I didn't have any friends to hang out with on a Friday afternoon so he took me there. I stayed close beside my Uncle Diego, afraid since I had seen Alex and his gang of friends hanging out near the concessions stand. Not too long after my uncle and I got to our seats, he decided to go get us some snacks. I had already scanned the area, knowing that Alex might be anywhere, and I saw that he wasn't near me so I thought I was safe, so I didn't feel bad when my uncle left me there to go get in line for candy. I should have gone with him. I shouldn't have been so stupid.

It didn't take long for me to realize how big of a mistake I had made. I was sitting there quietly, watching the marching band getting ready for their before game show, when I felt a horrible pain running down my back. It felt as if something was slowly dripping down my back, something boiling hot. I turned around to see Alex and his friends laughing at me, Alex holding a now empty plate that I could tell once had nachos on it. I figured out what happened very quickly, he had poured the hot cheese from his nachos down my back. The tears started forming in my eyes from the horrible pain, and they all saw it. It only made them laugh harder. I wanted to punch them all in the face, but I knew that they would overpower me, and I would get hurt worse than I could ever hurt them. As soon as they caught sight of my uncle, they ran off while I quickly pulled my jacket on over my now cheese covered shirt and back. I didn't want him to see what had happened. I could tell that he already thought I was pretty pathetic; I didn't want to make it any worse.

Throughout the game I sat there squirming, never able to get comfortable with that drying cheese on my back. I sat in the car smelling like bad cheese and as soon as I got home, I went into the bathroom and took off my jacket. That part was easy, the hard part was peeling off my shirt. With the cheese dried to my skin, I peeled it off slowly as I softly whimpered. Each time I pulled the shirt a bit more off of my body, the more burned skin it revealed and the more pain and embarrassment I felt. I spent at least two hours in the bathroom getting the cheese off and trying to sooth my skin that was so burned that it actually bubbled a little. I always kept that a secret from everyone. I didn't want anyone to know about how humiliated I felt. Alex didn't feel that way though. He has always showed off about every cruel thing he has ever done to anybody, especially me though. I can only hope that after tonight, things might change for the better.

Colomba and I make it to our seats in the stands, we are crowded on all sides by countless people. I am a bit nervous being trapped by so many people, but I try to enjoy myself as I watch Colomba looking at everything around her as if she is completely fascinated by every single thing. I smile when I see the life in her aquamarine eyes.

"Hey, I'll be back in just a second, okay?" She nods her head with a bright smile.

"Sure, I'll be right here." Without Alex around, I know that I am at least a little bit safer walking by myself in this crowd. I want to head to the concessions stand to get some chocolate covered raisins. I remember how much Colomba enjoys them and I think that she would appreciate it. I can only hope that she won't be too upset by what I have to do when the game starts. I have too much planned to let her presence get in the way. I will keep her safe, but I won't let this stop me.

Chapter Seventeen
Colomba-
Facing The
Bull-Y

Everyone is so tightly packed into the stands that it feels like I'm going to be smooshed at any second. Luis is sitting beside me, holding the box of chocolate covered raisins we are sharing. It was really sweet that Luis remembered how much I love these. He is such a good friend.

I think that a lot of people are here, not only because this is a big game, but also because they want to see if the Crow will do something else. I have to admit that those people are a little stupid. Why would you come to a place where you suspect a super villain might show up and you might get hurt? I came here to stop him; they came just to see the chaos. I guess that some people just don't have any sense.

The marching band is just getting on the field to start their before game show and the crowd around me roars with applause. While everyone else is focused on the band getting into place, I scan the crowd, looking for anything suspicious. Everyone seems to be acting normally; their eyes are glued to the band as they start to play a very fast paced song, nobody is stepping away from the stands to do anything, and everyone is just hanging out as if nothing unusual has happened today.

As I watch the crowd having fun, I start thinking that maybe I was wrong. Maybe the Crow isn't coming back tonight, and I've been worried about nothing. Maybe he will just let Alex return to his normal self, and everything will be alright. I let myself relax a little as the band finishes playing their song and the principal, AKA Angela's dad and the major of our town, goes onto the field, holding a microphone.

"Good evening everyone." The principal's voice echoes throughout the football field. His voice lacks any excitement or enthusiasm like you would expect at a game like this. His voice is very somber, like he's speaking at a funeral. "Thank you all very much for coming tonight. As most of you probably know, one of the players on the football team, Mr. Alex Donner, was taken over by the Crow earlier today. His whereabouts are currently unknown so I hope that all of you can join me in a moment of silence in the hope that Mr. Donner can be returned to us as soon as possible and this madman, the Crow, can be captured and brought to justice." Everyone bows their heads in the stands as an almost uncomfortable silence falls over the massive crowd. There is someone though who apparently isn't planning on showing any respect right now.

It starts off as a faint rumbling, as if a massive

thunderstorm is coming in from miles away, but there are no clouds in the starry sky. I lift my head to look around, trying to find where that strange sound could be coming from. My eyes stop scanning the area when I notice something that makes me narrow my eyes in confusion. The soda in the cup of the person sitting next to me is making ripples, as if something is making the earth shake. More people start looking around as the rumbling gets louder and louder. I stand up when I notice something that makes the hairs on the back of my neck stand up straight. The line of trees that stand behind the football field are shaking. I don't even have time to warn anybody before I massive shape leaps out from the trees with a mighty roar, making some of the trees break apart and crash to the ground in a heap of splinters, branches, and fallen leaves. The shape stops moving in the center of the football field and now we can all clearly see that the Crow's creature has come back, and it doesn't appear that he has come to be friendly.

The creature stands in the center of the field, glaring at everyone in the stands who stare back at him in absolute terror. The creature releases another roar and dozens upon dozens of people rush out of the stands and run to their cars while many others remain as still as statues in their fear. Before anyone around me can react, I run away as if I am terrified by what Alex has become. Of course, I'm not. I just need to be alone so that I can transform myself and kick this thing's butt. I hear Luis calling out my name in distress, and I feel someone grab my hand, but I just pull my hand out of their grip and run as fast as I can out of the crowd and behind the concessions stand where nobody else is. Before anybody can find me, I place my hand over my pin and say the magic words, "Peaceful warrior." I close my eyes and feel the rush of wind around me. As soon as it dies down, I know that I have become Silver Dove.

I open my wings out wide and take off into the sky. I head straight for the creature with determination. Below me, in the crowd, I can see people pointing up at me and cheering, but I don't pay any attention to them. I have work to do. The creature growls up at me as soon as it sees me. I land about twenty feet in front of it, making sure that I have enough room to get away if necessary. I try to make myself seem confident by standing tall in front of this creature when I really just want to get away as fast as possible. I clear my throat so that my voice can sound strong as I finally speak to this strange creature.

"Who are you supposed to be anyway!?" The creature growls at me before it answers me.

"Bull.... Y! Bull-Y!" It says these two words as if it is difficult for the creature to speak. As if it is a child first learning how to talk. Wow. When the Crow transformed Alex, he must have made him *really* stupid.

The Bull-Y quickly moves towards me and raises one of its massive fists up above me and I instantly know what it plans on doing. I lunge out of the way as the Bull-Y slams its fist on the ground, actually creating cracks in the football field from his power. My heart stops for a moment as I look at the cracks. He is just as strong as me! If he's as strong as me, he might be able to beat me!

I don't have a chance to think about how bad this is before the Bull-Y charges at me like… well, like a bull. It's horns are lowered, ready to try and impale me. I dodge the creature, unsheathe my sword, and strike down at the horn closest to me. All this does is make my sword shake like crazy from the force while it doesn't even look as if I did anything to him. The Bull-Y notices this and gives me a deep, evil laugh before it charges at me again, this time it has its arms out in front of it, so he can grab me. I lunge again and swipe my sword down at the creature's arm, but it doesn't even make a scratch on the creature's skin. Feeling desperate, I swing the sword at the creature's head, but that just makes a strange thunk sound from the impact. The creature laughs as if my attempts to defeat him are funny. I don't find it funny at all. There is no way that I can take down this creature by my own power, I need to try reasoning with it.

"Listen Alex," the Bull-Y doesn't even react when I call him by his real name. "You can't let the Crow control you like this. I know that you are still there buried underneath this creepy looking face. You have always been against the Crow, saying how much you hate him, so don't listen to him. I know he must have promised you something to make you accept these powers, but I bet that this isn't what you wanted. To get rid of them, all you have to do is willingly give up the powers and everything will return to normal, I promise. Please just trust me, and I will make sure that everything will be alright. You will be safe." I lower my sword in one hand and hold out my other hand to him, hoping that he will take it. I was wrong to hope for that.

The Bull-Y uses one of its massive hands to grab the hand I had been holding out to him, squeezing it so tightly that if I wasn't invincible, I know it would have broken. In the split second I have to think, I think about how much whatever he plans on doing is going to hurt. As soon as that thought passes through my mind, he swings me over his head by my hand and slams me onto the ground. He doesn't even give me a moment to breathe before he swings me over his head again and slams me onto the ground on the other side. My hands loosen and my sword tumbles out of my grip. I hear it fall a few feet away, but I can't grab it again before he starts swinging me and slamming me into the ground again, over and over. He does this so quickly that I can't even count how many times he has done this to me. I feel my body growing limp in exhaustion and the force he has been putting on me. He must have noticed this since he seems to get bored with slamming me on the ground. Instead of doing that, he throws me into the stands of the football field. I land with a crash on the metal stands, creating a massive dent in the seats where I fell.

I pick myself up, wobbling unsteadily on my feet. To keep myself from falling down, I gently fly in the air as I try to get my senses back after what just happened. There is no reasoning with this thing. Either the Crow has too much control over him, or the Crow just made him too stupid to understand sense. With all of the people that the Crow has transformed, I was able to talk them down and helped them understand things so that they willingly gave up their powers. I don't think that will work here.

I think back to the ways to get rid of these powers that my grandma once told me. Let's see, they could either willingly give up the powers, they could get so exhausted that the powers just go away, or they can get knocked out and the powers will leave them. Okay, so the first option is out, I definitely know that, I can still feel him slamming me against the ground from my attempt at doing that. I don't think the second option will do either since that would take forever and I think he would tire me out faster than I could tire him out. If I get exhausted faster, then I will transform back into my normal self and I can't let that happen. So that means that the only thing I can do is knock him out.

The only problem with that is that this thing seems to be pretty strong and not much can hurt it. I swung my sword at his head and he barely seemed to feel it. I know that I hit him pretty softly since I didn't want to hurt him, but that would have definitely hurt most people. No, I need to do something that will definitely get him down while also keeping myself safe. I don't want to get flung around again like a child's toy. I look around the football field to try and find some way to do what needs to be done. My eyes grow wide as an idea pops into my head and hope fills my heart, but then quickly leaves again when I realize the obvious. I know that I will need to get closer to that thing if I want to get it right. I only have one shot at this. I take a deep breath to get rid of my fear before I soar quickly toward the creature, getting ready to duck and dodge whatever strike he plans on hitting me with.

While the creature lifts an arm to try and knock me out of the air, I swerve out of the way and summon my sword to me. The sword seems to fly through the air on its own. It flies straight into my hand, but it doesn't stay there very long. As soon as I have a grip on it, I throw it as hard as I can, which in my Silver Dove form is pretty hard. The Bull-Y easily dodges my sword and chuckles darkly at me, amused that I missed him. A look of confusion passes over his face when I smile at him, he wasn't what I was aiming for.

Behind him, my sword flies straight at the pole that holds up the scoreboard for the game. My sword hits the pole just right, slicing through it completely. Using all of my speed, I fly out of the way. The Bull-Y cocks its head to the side in confusion. It doesn't have time to realize what happened before the scoreboard falls down directly on top of him with a mighty crash.

Dust and debris flies through the air from the scoreboard hitting the ground. I summon my sword back to me, just in case that force somehow didn't knock him out. I hold my sword out in front of me, prepared for an attack. As the dust settles, I slowly start moving forward toward the fallen scoreboard. I watch for any kind of movement, my eyes darting from one spot to another, my heart pounding in terror.

When I am standing right in front of the scoreboard, I hear a soft moan and I feel something large grab onto my ankle. I release a little shout of terror as I bring my sword up and hit the Bull-Y right in the middle of his forehead with the bottom of the handle of my sword. The Bull-Y releases another moan as he lets go of my ankle and closes his eyes. My final blow knocked him out. I quickly notice that most of his body is pinned underneath the fallen board. I quickly lift it off of him and toss it aside just as his body changes from that hideous creature, back to the guy he used to be, Alex.

Kneeling beside him, I place my hand on his cheek to turn his head to face me. He doesn't look as if he was harmed by what happened. As I am examining him, he quickly opens his eyes and I practically jump away from him, worried that he might recognize me behind my mask if I let him look me that close up. He stares up at me in shock.

"What just happened? Is the Crow gone?" He picks himself up so that he is in a sitting position as he frantically looks around, scared to death that he will find the Crow lurking around somewhere. It's almost strange to see the guy who always acts so strong and sure of himself acting so scared. I have to control myself to make sure that I don't laugh or chuckle at him.

"It's alright. The Crow is gone." His wild eyes look at me in absolute horror. What did the Crow do to him?

"Are you sure that he's gone?" I nod my head and smile at him, trying to be comforting.

"Yes, I am sure. You are safe now." He quickly grabs my hand, as if terrified that I will leave him.

"Did I hurt anybody?" I blink a few times, almost shocked to hear him be so concerned about other people. He is usually so self-absorbed to even notice the other people around him, unless they are the ones he is showing off to, of course.

"No, you didn't hurt anybody. Did the Crow tell you to hurt people?" He shakes his head, his eyes still wild looking in fear.

"No, no, he just wanted me to scare people. I'm afraid that I might have hurt a girl named Colomba. Do you know her? Is she alright?" My heart melts in my chest when I hear his concern for me. Wow, I never realized that he does actually care about me, even just a little. I've been thinking for a while now that Alex was only interested in me because I'm pretty. Now though, it kind of looks like he really does care.

"Yes, I know who she is, and she is fine." He releases a sigh of relief and the crazy look in his eyes quickly fades away.

"Good, real good. The Crow promised me power so that I could win the game tonight. He didn't tell me that he would control me though. He said that he wanted me to scare everyone, but he really wanted me to scare her." My attention is immediately caught by what he just said.

"What do you mean he really wanted you to scare her?"

"Yeah, he told me to scare her specifically. He said he…" He lets his words trail off while an uncomfortable look comes over his face. He chews on his bottom lip, something I know he does whenever he has said, or was about to say, something he knows would upset me to hear.

"What did he say Alex?" My voice is firm, and he pauses for a second, knowing that he has to tell me.

"He said that he wanted me to show her what I really am, a monster." I have to stare at him for a moment to see if he is messing with me or not. He isn't.

"Why did he want you to scare her specifically Alex?" He shrugs his shoulders at me.

"I don't know, he told me to scare her, but not to mess with anyone trying to rescue her. He wanted her to be safe, but scared." What is going on? Why was the Crow singling me out? Alex said that the Crow wanted me to see Alex as a monster, why? Why is the Crow so interested in how I feel about Alex? Why am I so important to him? I look at Alex, and I can tell by just looking at him that he no longer wants to answer any of my questions. I need to leave him be.

"Alright Alex, thank you very much for answering my questions. You better get ready though, if you want to play in this game you will have to get changed into your gear quickly. They won't want to wait all night for you." His eyes light up in excitement, almost like a small child entering an amusement park.

"You mean that they haven't started without me?" I smile as a small chuckle escapes me, amused by the eagerness shining in his eyes.

"Nope, you came in right before they were about to start. You can go ahead and get ready while I find everyone and tell them that everything is alright now." He nods at me before running off without another word to the locker room so that he can change.

I watch him for a moment, happy that he is back to his normal self and that he is happy. Things may have been bad for us for a while, but I am still happy knowing that he is happy too. I open my wings and take off into the dark sky. My eyes scan over the area to see if I can find where everyone went to. It doesn't take me long to spot the massive crowd of people standing in the parking lot beside the football field. They had probably been watching the entire battle in safety from there. I smile as I fly over to them as fast as I can. The entire crowd breaks into a roaring cheer when I get close to them and I have to wait a moment before they fall silent so that I can speak.

"Everyone, Alex Donner is now alright and is willing and able to take part in the game tonight!" The crowd cheers again, but they get quiet when I hold up my hand to them. "We are all safe for now but remember that the Crow is still with us! You must make sure that you look out for each other! He preys on those who have pain in their hearts! Don't let anyone feel as if they are alone, if you don't then we will all suffer with them! I will leave you for now, but I will be back in case the Crow decides to return!" I turn away from them to face the football field with its massive amount of destruction with the ripped-up grass, broken stands, and the scoreboard that I knocked to the ground. I place my hand over the dove on my breast plate and say the magic words, "Bring peace little dove." The dove flies off my armor and into the sky, almost looking like a new star in the darkness. It slowly begins to glow, and everyone has to turn their faces away from its brightness. It is so bright that it almost looks as if the night has been replaced instantly with day. When we can no longer feel the warmth of the light, we open our eyes to see that all of the damage from the fight has disappeared and I know that all the destruction in the school from earlier today is now gone as well.

A huge smile comes over my face as I fly off into the darkness with the crowd cheering behind me as they make their way back to their seats so that the game can finally begin. I fly into a group of trees not too far away from the football field, but still far enough away so that nobody can see me transform back into my usual self. I need to hurry so that I can find Luis and the two of us can get back to our seats and watch the game. I may not really like sports, but I will be happy to see Alex playing, back to his regular self.

Chapter Eighteen
Luis-
The Truth

It wasn't too long after I walked back into the stands that I found Colomba again. Apparently, she had hidden behind a shed where they hold all the lawn care equipment for the football field during the battle. I was just glad to see that she wasn't hurt. The two of us are sitting in the stands now, watching the last minute of the game. Our school's team is only a point behind, and I'm not happy to admit that Alex is the one who got most of those points. I watch the game, not entirely sure what is going on since I never bothered to learn the rules of football because I hate the sport with every fiber of my being. Most of that remaining minute ticks by as Alex catches the ball that someone on the opposite team threw and he runs to one side of the field. The people around us start cheering so I'm guessing that's a good thing. He almost makes it to the other side before someone on the other team tackles him to the ground. While everyone around me boos and lets out moans of disappointment, I have to hold back a smile after watching him hit the ground so hard.

One of the coaches calls a time out and both teams huddle up. I glance up at the clock on the scoreboard again to see that only fifteen seconds are left in the game and everyone is chatting excitedly to each other. The people around me say that he only has about ten yards to go, whatever that means. When I glance over at Colomba I can tell that she's just as clueless as me about what's going on since she's glancing around the field with scrutinizing eyes, as if she is trying to figure out what's going on by observing the players during the time out.

The coach ends the time out and the players return to their positions while everyone watches eagerly, hoping that our team wins, while I hope that they lose. The players move into action and the ball is quickly passed to Alex who starts sprinting around every player around him, trying to get the ball to the end of the field. Many of the people in the stands leap to their feet and cheer so loudly that I cover my ears. Only a few seconds are left, and it almost looks as if Alex is going to make it, until one player gets in his way. He was only a few feet from crossing to the end of the field when another player tackled him just as the final second ticked away leaving our team one point behind. We lost.

All the people who had been cheering only moments before are now groaning in frustration. They grab their stuff with angry snatching fingers and march out of the stands to head to their cars. While they all grumble to each other, I keep myself from laughing as I hide a smile behind my hand.

Colomba looks a little upset by our team's loss, but she isn't heartbroken like everyone else. The two of us start making our way through the crowd to head towards the parking lot for her grandmother and my uncle to pick us up.

As I look at her, I think about why I made all of this happen. She told me that she had to reschedule our time for painting that portrait for the doctor so that she could be with Alex. I knew what that meant, she was going out on a date with him. I couldn't let that happen. In the end, Alex would only end up hurting her. Even though I did it to protect her, I still feel as if I should say something, apologize to her in some way about how things turned out. I clear my throat softly.

"Colomba, I'm really sorry that all this stuff happened to you today. I mean with getting tossed by that monster and having to break off your date with Alex after school today."

"Our date? What are you talking about?" Colomba looks at me as if I have suddenly sprouted trees out of my ears.

"Your date. You said that you were meeting up with Alex after school, so I-" Colomba surprises me by laughing.

"We weren't," she stops for a moment to release a giggle, "on a date. He was one of the people I was assigned to tutor in math." My eyes open wide in surprise. I feel like an idiot, but it still feels like a can fly in happiness, so I guess you could call me a happy idiot. She shakes her head at how silly I sounded while she continues to giggle. "Trust me, I wouldn't date that guy if he was the last man on earth. I have better ways of spending my time than listening to some guy show off about how great he is. He is also just a jerk. I would have to be nuts to go on a date with him." She giggles again while I laugh with her. Wow I kind of screwed up today. I transformed a guy for no reason apparently. Well, I guess he did deserve it after everything else he has done to me and everybody else, but I transformed him because I wanted to show Colomba how everyone else views him. I wanted her to view him as a monster, but I guess that she already sees him that way. I did all that, went through all that trouble, for nothing. I am probably the biggest idiot in this town tonight. Colomba lets out a little groan of annoyance.

"I left my sweater where we were sitting. I'll be right back." She runs off back the way we came, and I wait patiently for her. A minute ticks by before a sudden feeling in my gut tells me to move closer to the concessions stand. I don't know why I feel this way, but I walk over to it and stay there for a moment to find a man that looks very familiar walking toward Alex who is still in his jersey and gear, and who had apparently just walked off the field. I recognize this older man since I have been going to school with Alex for so long, he is Alex's dad. He is a tall man, but still an inch or two shorter than me, so around six feet tall. Even though he is about as tall as me, he is not as skinny as me. This guy has a bit of a belly sticking out over his belt that jiggles a little underneath his T-shirt as he walks. Some stubble covers his face as if he has forgotten to shave for a couple days in a row. A baseball cap covers his head, but if it was off, I know that I would see a nearly completely bald head. Judging from how he still has that proud posture and the swagger that Alex always has, I'm guessing he used to be considered attractive. Now though, not so much. His clothes are nice, but not very clean. It's almost as if he has enough money to dress well but doesn't care enough to maintain what he has.

I notice that when Alex sees his father, he straightens his back and his eyes suddenly look worried. My eyes narrow in confusion as I watch this sudden change come over Alex. What is going on here?

"Hello Sir." Alex says this with a strong, serious voice, but I can hear something hidden behind his voice. Is that… fear?

"What was that?" Alex's dad growls down at him, his eyes burning with rage.

"What was what, Sir?" Alex asks while I see his knees beginning to tremble beneath him. The question only makes Alex's dad even more angry.

"What was with that performance tonight? Your team lost! You failed them!" My eyes grow wide from where I am watching them, glad that neither of them can see me. Alex stares at his father with a hurt, shocked expression.

"But Dad, I got practically every point my team made. I'm the reason we did as good as we did." Alex doesn't sound the way he usually does. There is no confidence in his voice, no pride. Right now, all I can hear is misery and pain.

"*Good?*" Alex's dad chuckles coldly,

almost the exact same way Alex does whenever he's about to do something cruel to me. "Oh please. You were all pathetic, but especially *you*. You are supposed to be the one to carry the team, but you're just a plain, pathetic loser. I don't understand how you have the nerve to go out in public when you're such a pitiful little creep. You should just walk home, maybe that will put some muscle on that wimpy little body of yours." He considers his son's body wimpy? His arms are as thick as a small tree trunk while mine are so weak that if I tried to lift any weights my arms would probably break. I wonder what Alex's dad would say about my scrawny body. Alex looks at his father with astonishment.

"But our house is two miles from here, and it's nighttime. You want me to walk home in the dark?" Alex's dad's glare somehow grows even darker than before. I think I can even see Alex quiver a little bit in fright at the sight of it. I don't blame him. I'm terrified right now and I'm not even the one this guy is angry at.

"Yes, yes I do. Maybe after that you'll gain a bit of a spine. I think that everyone can see that you need it. We will talk about this more when you get home." Without another word, Alex's dad leaves him alone, leaving both Alex and me very surprised. I also see something else that I have never seen before on Alex's face, terror. Alex's eyes are wide, and his shoulders are tense as he stares after his father while his hands quiver at his side. He is terrified of going home. I don't even need the power to read minds to realize what he is thinking. He is silently hoping that he will get home *after* his father has already gone to bed so that he won't have to deal with him when he gets there. I find myself hoping for the same thing too. I am somehow afraid for my worst enemy. Afraid of what might happen to him when he gets home.

Oh my gosh. That's what he has to go home to every day? As I watch Alex stare after his dad in pain, I sort of understand why he is the way he is. His dad didn't even mention anything about how Alex got transformed into a giant monster. It's almost as if that doesn't matter to him. He didn't ask if he was okay or if he wanted to talk about it. All he cared about was that Alex's team lost and he blamed it on Alex even though he did so much better than everyone else. I don't think Alex could ever do anything that would be good enough for his dad. Alex may be popular at school and have all the money in the world, but when he goes home, he is stuck in that house with his worst enemies, his father and himself.

Alex seems to snap out of the shock of his father leaving him to walk home alone at night since he picks up his bag of football equipment and starts walking away. I can't help but notice that the bag looks very heavy. Maybe I should offer to help him carry some of the stuff or ask my uncle if he can give Alex a ride home… maybe I should… No, no I can't do that. Even if Alex does want some help, he would never accept it from me. He would think it is weak to accept help from the guy he is always calling a pathetic loser, just like how his dad was calling him that.

I watch him walk away from me for a moment, completely surprised by a new feeling that I've never had for him before. Pity. I pity Alex right now. After everything he has done to me, I pity the person I think of as a monster.

As I watch him walk away, Alex kicks at a soda can as he walks past it. His anger furrows his brows and his eyes stare ahead, looking at everything with bitter hatred, as if everything in the world has done something terrible to him and he wants revenge. I walk away too, in the opposite direction though. I'm smart enough to know that if I go anywhere near Alex right now then he might beat the snot out of me. It makes me feel kind of pathetic to be avoiding him like this, but it will be worth it if I get out of here without any injuries. I look back at Alex one last time before I turn around again, feeling sympathy toward him for the first time in my life.

I always thought that if I saw Alex being hurt then I would be happy. I couldn't have been more wrong. Right now, I almost feel guilty for what I did to him today. I hurt someone who is being bullied too, I just didn't know it. Unlike me, Alex is popular at school, but the bullied kid at home. I guess Alex has a lot of anger built up inside of him, but it doesn't give him the excuse to hurt me and the other kids in this school all the time. There is no excuse for something like that. There is no excuse and there is no forgiveness. I silently make my way around Alex so that I can wait for Colomba to get back. She is taking a while just to get her sweater. I wait patiently though to make sure that the two of us can wait for our rides together.

Chapter Nineteen
Colomba-
A New Point
Of View

From behind the concessions stand, I watch as Alex's father leaves him to walk home alone while I stare at Alex with pity in my heart and tears forming in my eyes. His father is marching away from him in absolute rage while Alex just looks at him with misery. I can't believe what I just saw. How could Alex's own father say something so cruel? It's normal for a parent to be a little upset that their child didn't win a game they worked so hard for, but that was way over the top. What is *wrong* with that guy? How could a father say something like that to their child? My dad would never say something like that to me, and he would be furious at anybody who would even try to say it.

Alex just watches his father until he is out of sight before he turns around to start walking in the opposite direction. Alex's eyes are lacking any emotion. It's almost as if his father removed his soul with his horrible words. His head is usually held high in pride, but right now his head is down and his shoulders are hunched forward. My heart breaks when I suddenly realize who he reminds me of with his changed body posture and the pain in his eyes, Luis.

Whenever I see Luis when he is alone, he always looks as if the entire world is trying to beat him down, and the world is slowly succeeding. I want to talk to him about it, but when I ask Luis about it, he always says that he is fine. I don't know what I can do to help my friend, but I'll do anything to see him smile. I almost feel that way about Alex right now, I want to help him. I can't stand seeing anyone look so miserable. No matter who they are, I feel like I have to help them.

I was too busy thinking about how much I pity Alex that I didn't even bother to realize that he is walking toward me and he doesn't know it since I am hidden behind the building, and he also probably doesn't want to talk to me after what just happened. He turns around the corner and almost walks directly into me. Alex leaps back in surprise when he sees me, and his usual confidence returns to him in an instant.

"Hey girl, how are you doing? I'm glad you came to see me play. Too bad my team sucks though. If it wasn't for them being so lazy out there, we would have won." I smile at him, trying to make it seem like I didn't hear anything he and his father said to each other. He already lost the game; I don't want to make him feel worse about himself.

"I'm alright, thanks for asking. I really am sorry that you guys didn't win. And I'm also sorry about everything that happened to you with the Crow today. That must have been a horrible experience." Alex just chuckles, as if my concern for him is silly.

"I was okay, not even he can keep me down forever. I'm just sorry that I hurt you while I was under his control." He gently places his hands at the tops of my arms, right where it meets the shoulder. I know that this should be a comforting gesture, but with his massive hands on my tiny body it almost feels as if he is restraining me, as if he is keeping me captive with those huge hands. Something about this gesture makes me feel very uncomfortable, I suppose it is because he is trying to be romantic, but it only makes me nervous. "You know that I would never hurt you, right?" He gazes into my eyes and it almost feels as if he is a predator trying to observe its prey, trying to find a weakness. I give him a gentle smile, trying to relieve some of my tension.

"Of course, I know that. I could never think of you as someone who would hurt me." My voice comes out a little shaky in my discomfort, but Alex doesn't seem to notice or care. He just smiles at me with delight.

"That's fantastic. You know, I'm pretty free right now. If you like, we can go grab a burger or something at the Captain's Ship. That diner has the best burgers, and I'll even buy you a shake there. What do you say?" I want to say that I would rather jump in a shark tank than go on a date with him, but I don't want to hurt him after what I just saw. As my dad would say, that would just be pouring salt in the wound. Now that I understand what he is going through, I can't just hurt him as if it is nothing. I can't be heartless.

"Well I can't hang out now, my grandmother is picking me up in a few minutes." He lowers his eyes in disappointment. I have made his already terrible day even worse. I don't even think as I say something else. "But I am free to talk at school on Monday if you want." He immediately perks up and his smile returns in full vengeance. His teeth sparkle and his handsome face lights up with joy.

"Great, then I will see you on Monday. I'll be looking for you." He gives me a quick wink before turning around and walking away, probably to head home.

I watch him for a moment, my stomach instantly feeling sick at the sight of that wink. I shouldn't have done that. The reason I stopped talking to him was because I realized how big of a jerk he is, and I didn't want to get involved. Now that I know what he goes through at home though, I kind of understand why he acts like he does. He is secretly miserable on the inside while he makes himself look cool and collected on the outside. He puts others down so that he can feel better since his dad always makes him feel terrible about himself. Is it the right thing to do to make yourself feel better? Absolutely not, but I'm pretty sure that Alex could use a friend, and not just one who wants to be around him since he is considered popular.

I walk over to Luis and the two of us chat a little as we wait for our rides. It doesn't take long for my grandmother's car to pull up and I eagerly get inside, so happy to be getting away from Alex and everything that has happened tonight. I don't know why, but I have always loved my grandma's car. It is one of those old-fashioned station wagons that she has had since before I was born. It is an old car, and its age can definitely be seen. A purple stain practically covers one of the seats in the back from when I dumped my grape juice on it when I was four years old, the radio still has a cassette player from when those were actually a thing, and one of the knobs on the AC is broken so we have to turn it just the right way to turn it off so we don't freeze to death during the winter. It is an old car, but one that I love. Hanging from the rearview mirror is a little glass Christmas ornament of a dove. My grandmother has dove things spread all over the house, but this is one of my favorites.

Before my grandma can bombard me with endless questions about what happened tonight, I stretch as far as I can in the cramped space. After all the excitement from that battle, I just want to pass out and not wake up for a couple days. I will sleep well tonight. My grandma smiles warmly at me, helping relieve some of the gloom I felt after watching Alex with his dad.

"Considering I just drove past Alex I'm guessing that everything is back to normal." I smile back at her, feeling her pride in me like a wave of warmth coming over me.

"Yep, all is right with the world." I spend the next ten minutes of the car ride home telling her about that battle and everything that happened afterward; the team losing, what happened with Alex and his dad, and all my thoughts concerning everything. When I am done talking, I am practically breathless since I said everything so quickly in my excitement, but now I am also a bit angry because I am thinking about everything that the Crow did and it somehow connects back to me.

"There are so many things that I don't understand about what happened today. Like why could Luis get the Bull-Y to let go of me when I could barely even hurt him as Silver Dove with my super strength? And why did the Crow want to change Alex instead of one of the bullied kids? I don't understand." I moan as I bend my head back and rub my eyes. It has been a long day.

"For your first question," my grandma says in her usual calm, sweet voice, "maybe Luis was able to do something because the Crow told Alex not to harm anyone trying to rescue you. Alex also told you that the Crow didn't want to harm you, only to scare you. So maybe he just ordered the Bull-Y to pretend that Luis hurt him so that he could let you go without anyone asking questions. And for your second question, you kind of answered it yourself. The Crow said that he wanted to show you, and everyone else, how he viewed Alex. As a monster. So he decided to change him instead of one of the bullied kids so that he could get his point across." I turn my head back to look at her as she drives through the dark country around us.

"But why does he want to show everyone that?" She smiles softly with sadness clouding her eyes.

"I believe that this young man does have a good heart, or else the medal wouldn't have worked for him, but he has a broken soul. Having a good heart but a broken soul can lead to many problems. You want to try and do what is right, but you are filled with so much pain and misery that you sometimes let that get in the way of what you hope to do. With the Crow, he wants to make the school a more pleasant place for everyone. That is something to be admired about him. But he has also experienced a lot of pain because of the people in this school, especially Alex it seems. He lets his hatred invade his mind and that helps hurt his decisions. Maybe his anger led him to make this decision to transform Alex to make everyone see him that way." I stay silent for a moment to let her words sink in, but then I finally ask the question that is really eating away at my mind.

"Why did he want to do that for me though? Alex said that the Crow wanted me specifically to know that. Why? Does the Crow have a crush on me or something? Does he really care about me like that?" She suddenly looks away from me, as if she's uncomfortable by what I just said.

"I don't know. I do not know this young man, so I can't answer for him." Something tells me though that she does know something. She is looking ahead at the road in front of us, but there is a look in her eyes that tells me that something is wrong. It almost feels as if she is hiding something from me, but she never hides anything from me. I mean she kept the whole Silver Dove thing a secret from me for the longest time, but she eventually told me when she thought it was the right time. We have never kept secrets from each other, what is different now? What is she keeping from me?

The rest of the car ride is spent in silence, the two of us lost in our own thoughts. I'm not sure what she is thinking, but my mind is full, trying to understand what she is hiding from me.

Chapter Twenty
Luis-
Pain Inside

It is pitch black outside except for the faint, eerie glow of a streetlamp that is flickering on the street below me. I look out my window from the second-floor apartment that my uncle and I share above his shop. Shadow is calmly cleaning her feathers with her beak while we sit in silence. The two of us are very comfortable with silence. I suppose I am so comfortable with silence since most people in school have never included me in their conversations, so I am used to being alone.

When I get bored of staring out the window, I grab the TV remote off the dresser beside me and turn on the television. The news pops up immediately. The news anchor is sitting at a desk while in the top right corner of the screen she is showing video footage of something. I look a little closer to realize what she is actually showing everyone, and I feel my hand tighten around the remote in my controlled fury. It is a recording of the battle between the Bull-Y and Silver Dove. As I watch the footage, Silver Dove throws her sword at the scoreboard, which falls right on top of the Bull-Y, ending the battle.

"This was the scene earlier tonight at the football game at Drew's Hollow High School. The Crow struck once again and transformed one of the football players, who then caused havoc before Silver Dove arrived. She was able to defeat the creature, and everything returned to normal. The adolescent who was transformed had this to say." The screen changes to show Alex with a reporter, the reporter has a microphone in front of Alex's face. Even though I would be incredibly uncomfortable having to talk to someone on TV, Alex seems to be loving it. His smile practically takes over his face, and his eyes have that usual confidence in his glance that makes him seem uninterested in what is going on, as if he gets interviewed every day. But after years of knowing him I know that he is bursting with excitement. He is still wearing his jersey in the interview, so they must have done this right after the game while he was still on the field.

"Yeah, the Crow forced me to be like that. He said that he wanted to bring as much fear to my school as possible, so he decided to transform the one person that everyone looks up to, me. He thought that he could defeat me, but because of Silver Dove that will never happen. Because of people like her and me, the Crow will one day be defeated. I hope that I can be the one to finally take him down." I press the off button as hard as I can in rage. That idiot actually thinks that everyone looks up to him? He deserves to have something even worse happen to him than just being transformed into a monster. One day I will figure out the perfect punishment for him, but for right now I just want to forget what I saw on the television. I want to forget everything that happened tonight. Well, except the part when I found out that he and Colomba weren't going on a date, that I will keep in my head forever.

There are several questions running through my mind and there is only one person on this earth who can answer them. I haven't spoken to her in a long time, but I must know. I place my hand on top of the Crow Medal and Shadow instantly stops grooming her feathers to look at me with curiosity.

"Speak to Silver Dove." Shadow immediately flies off her perch and soars into the medal. I feel my mind open up and I feel myself in the presence of my enemy.

Hello Silver Dove. I can hear the panic racing through her mind as she hears my voice. That panic quickly morphs into rage.

What do you want? Her voice in my mind is full of hatred and anger. She doesn't want to talk to me, but I don't care about what she wants. I want answers and I'm going to get them.

We need to talk. You got in my way tonight. Everyone knows what Alex is truly like and I was showing that to the world, but you had to come in and ruin everything. You must know what Alex is like if you go to my school, so why did you get in the way? I want to know this because I can't figure out why she would even want to help someone like him. I bet that a lot of people liked what I did to Alex. They probably didn't say anything out loud because that would make them look bad, but they definitely thought it. I mean, who wouldn't want to see the person who hurts everyone get what they deserve? Apparently, Silver Dove is one of the people who disagrees with me.

Of course I got in your way. You had him rampaging all over the place. I had to stop him to make sure that nobody got hurt. Yes, I do know that Alex can be a handful, but that doesn't mean that you have to hurt him. Of course, she's getting on her high horse making me sound like the bad guy. I'm the bad guy even though she's getting in the way of real justice.

You don't understand. You think that everything will turn out okay no matter what. It may work like that in your world, but not in mine and many other people's. I just want everyone to see him like that so that they can stop treating him like a god and possibly stop following his lead and hurting other people. I can hear her chuckle in my mind and my hands tighten into fists at my side.

You say that you wanted to do this to change people's minds. Are you sure it wasn't just Colomba's mind that you wanted to change? My heart seems to stop in my chest at her words. *Alex told me what you said in his head. You wanted to scare Colomba specifically. Why did you want her to see him like that? Why is her opinion so important to you?* My rage boils over and I scream at her through my mind.

That is none of your concern! Her rage must equal mine, because she screams right back at me so loudly that my head hurts.

I think it is Crow! If you are targeting anyone in my school, then I will get involved! You may have something against Alex, but that doesn't mean that you can just use your powers against him! You need to really think about what you are doing and decide if this is what you have to do to get what you want!

I cut off the connection between the two of us, not wanting to hear her voice any longer. How dare she bring Colomba up, that is none of her business. Shadow flies out of the medal and perches on top of my dresser. She looks at me for a moment, her dark eyes evaluating me, before she speaks.

"That sounded like a very stressful

conversation. I'm sorry that you had to go through with that. You wanted answers, but all you got was just as much anger as you gave her." I glare at her, feeling all of my frustration from my conversation being directed at her.

"Oh shut up Shadow! You think you're so smart, but you don't know anything about what's going on! Everything seems to be flipped around from what I thought it was!" Shadow doesn't even seem remotely upset even though I am yelling at her. She is just as serene as usual.

"Then explain it to me. Why is everything "flipped around"?" I release a sigh, getting rid of some of my anger. I try to think of the best way to explain my confusion, and my words are said in a monotone, as if my soul is leaking out of me with each word.

"I had the mission of transforming bullied kids. I thought that Alex would be the exception, but I was wrong. He is a bullied kid, it's just that his bully is at home while most peoples are at school." It actually hurts me to say that out loud. I was wrong about Alex. I always thought of him as someone who hurts people just because he enjoys it. Now I know that he hurts others because he is in pain too. Shadow simply nods her head at my words as if she somehow knows exactly how I feel.

"It must be a very difficult thing for you to say that you were wrong about Alex. I am very sorry that you have this confusing puzzle to deal with. You have to figure out how you should feel about Alex now that you know what his life is truly like." My anger returns to me and I glare with as much fire as I can into her calm black eyes.

"You think that I'm confused about how I should feel about Alex? No, I know exactly how I should feel! Just because somebody hurts him doesn't mean that he can use all the power he has to hurt everyone else."

"You mean like you do with your powers?" I look back at Shadow with wide eyes. I can't believe she just said that to me. She used to say stuff like that to me all the time, but she said that she would stop and work with me. For a while now she has kept that promise, but now there she stands on my dresser, staring at me as if she has done nothing wrong.

I open my mouth to say something mean to her, but then I stop and think about what she said. Am I acting just like Alex? Am I using my powers just because I have been hurt before? Maybe she's right, maybe… No, no I am not using my powers like that. I saw that there is a problem at my school, and I am trying to fix it. Nobody else is fixing the problem so I decided to take on that responsibility myself. Sure, I may be doing it in a way that might frighten some people, but they need to learn the lesson that I am trying to teach. You can't mess with other people without having some kind of punishment. I have been hurt, and I am enjoying what I am doing as the Crow for the most part, but I am not like Alex. I will never be like that monster.

Instead of responding to Shadow with anger, I look away from her to stare out my darkened window again as I silently place my hand over my Crow Medal, which sends Shadow back inside that medal so that I can be alone. I stare out the window while my heart feels heavy. There are no stars in the sky right now because it is cloudy out, I can't even see the moon, making the world seem just as dark as my heart.

Chapter Twenty- One
Colomba-
The Haunting
Dream

I lay in bed, tossing and turning as I replay everything that happened tonight, especially the conversation I had with the Crow in my head. After all this time, why did he decide to talk to me again now? He's always let the people he has possessed do the talking for him, but not today. What was different about today that made him do this? Was it because I got in his way of hurting Alex? Or was it because he wasn't able to complete his mission of changing my mind about Alex, his mission of making me see him as a monster. Maybe he just wanted to get in contact with me because he wanted answers to those questions he kept asking me. I hope I gave him the answers he wasn't looking for because he certainly didn't give me any of the answers I wanted.

When I asked him why he was so interested in me he practically exploded, saying it was "none of your concern". Why was he so defensive about that? I think about something I had said earlier to my grandmother while we were in the car. What if the Crow has a crush on me? Is that why he is so interested in changing my mind about Alex? Did the Crow somehow start thinking that I was getting too close to Alex and he got jealous so he decided to hurt Alex in the only way he could? I can only shiver in fear at the thought of the Crow having a crush on me. What would it be like to have someone so disturbed liking me that much?

I know that if he likes me enough to transform someone who he only thinks I am getting close to, then what would he do if I ever dated anyone that isn't him? I don't plan on dating anyone while I am in high school since I want to focus on my studies and go to a good college so I can become a doctor like my mother, but that thought still scares me. What would he do to any boy that would dare to date me? Would the Crow transform him into a hideous monster like he did with Alex or would he do something worse? I shudder at the thought of the other things the Crow could do. The Crow could transform someone and make them attack him, or the Crow could make a bunch of his demon dogs and have them attack him. My eyes grow wide as I stare up at the ceiling in horror at one thought that makes my heart jump in my chest. Would someone as insane as the Crow actually kill whoever I try to date? I take in several panicked breaths before I get myself under control. That hasn't happened and I won't let it happen. If I ever do date someone, I will protect them with every power I have to make sure that the Crow won't harm a hair on their head. I couldn't bear to live with myself if someone got hurt just because they cared about me.

Another thought invades my mind and I have to hold back a moan of misery. What if he tries to force me to be with him? A guy as disturbed as him might do that, it wouldn't surprise me. I would never let that happen, but I can only imagine how horrible it would be. If I didn't have my powers as Silver Dove, that might actually be an easy thing for him to do. All he would have to do is threaten my family or friends and I would do anything he wanted. There's no doubt that he would be the worst boyfriend ever. Judging from how he transformed Alex just for being close to me, I'm guessing that the Crow would be a super jealous boyfriend and would hate having anybody get close to me. I would go just as crazy as him if I ever dated him.

I close my eyes as I try to let my mind go quiet so that I can get some sleep. I probably spend another hour rolling over and over as I try to get myself comfortable and get rid of those terrible thoughts that seem to keep repeating in my head about the Crow before my eyes close and sleep finally comes to me. Even though I now have the rest that I tried so hard to get, it is not peaceful. As soon as my eyes have closed, I am in the middle of a dream.

I am flying through the clouds on a bright, beautiful day. The sun is shining above me, and white, fluffy clouds are floating around me. I am not flying in my Silver Dove form though. I am an actual dove. I am a little bird gently fluttering my wings through the air. Even while dreaming I realize that I have had a dream like this before. It was the night after I dealt with the Sprinter, I had a dream almost just like this. Just like in that dream, I land within the courtyard of an old building.

Within the center of the courtyard is a fountain with a statue of three people on it, a girl and two boys, all of them with a different kind of bird perched on their shoulders. Flowers grow along the perimeter of the courtyard and roses travel up the walls on strong vines. The perfume of these flowers almost makes me dizzy, but I don't pay any attention to the flowers or the fountain. My complete attention is drawn toward a small figure perched beneath the swaying branches of a weeping willow tree. My clever wings navigate me through the branches that swing in the faint breeze and I land in front of the figure.

Sitting in front of me is a crow. Since I am a tiny dove, the large crow stands tall over me, almost twice as big as I am. Even though this could be considered menacing to most people, I find a bit of comfort in it, as if I know that the crow can protect me if I need it to. This crow is my enemy and my friend. I know that I shouldn't trust this creature, but I know that the crow will never hurt me. The crow cares for me too much to do that. The crow would rather die than hurt me in any way. I don't know how I know this; I just do.

The crow seems very happy to see me, it lets out a caw of joy as it hops over and lowers its neck so that it can wrap its head around me, as if it is trying to hug me without arms. In my little dove form, I nuzzle my head into its dark feathers, enjoying the feeling of the crow's embrace. It is a peaceful moment, but the moment is cut short.

A shadow blocks out the sunlight above us for a second and the two of us glance up to see some large creature flying over us, circling slowly in the sky. I can't tell what it is since the sun is directly behind it and it is too bright for me to look at directly. The crow hops between me and the creature above us, spreading out its wings in front of me, shielding me from whatever it is. The crow glances back at me for a moment and gives me a faint caw. I somehow realize that it is trying to comfort me, to tell me that everything will be alright. I don't think that the crow believes that everything will be alright though. The feathers on the crow's wings are shaking even though there is no breeze and it isn't even remotely cold in this garden. The crow is shivering in fear because of that strange figure in the sky. Even though it is trying to comfort me, it is afraid too. I don't know what the shadow is above us, but I believe that the crow knows and is terrified.

I glance back up into the sky at the shadow. As I watch it, the creature circling above us seems to be getting larger by the second. My terror grows when I realize the obvious, the creature is coming right toward us. Whatever it is crashes through the swaying willow branches around us and lands on the ground, its massive wings practically blocking out the sun. This thing is probably five times bigger than the crow in front of me, making it around ten times larger than me in my tiny little dove form. I stare up at it, yet I still can't figure out what it is. It is only a figure of gloom, covered in shadows. All I know is that I am both afraid of it, as well as drawn to it. I want to get closer to this creature. I have the same feeling toward it that I do with the crow. I know that it is my enemy as well as my friend, but something about this strange shadow in front of me gives me more fear than the crow. Even though I know that this creature will not hurt me, I am still afraid. Even though this creature would also rather die than hurt me, I know that it will do anything to get what it wants.

The creature seems to evaluate us, staring at us calmly while we stare at it with our feathers quivering. My tiny heart is beating so fast that it almost sounds like rain beating down on a roof. My heartbeat is so quick that I am almost afraid that I will pass out or something. I don't have time for that though. The creature seems to get bored looking at us since it opens up its massive wings and lunges forward. Huge claws on what look like shriveled hands reach out for the crow and me. An earsplitting screech comes from the creature almost sounding like the cry of a demented animal. The crow lets out a loud caw of warning, but the creature doesn't care. It just keeps coming at us with full force.

I can almost feel its claws around me before I take in a huge gasp of air and I sit up straight in my bed. I glance around in terror, expecting to see some monster coming to get me in my sleep. I take in a few quick gasps of air as I try to calm myself. It was just a dream. It was a dream you idiot so stop acting like it really happened. You weren't getting attacked by some giant creature, you were asleep. You are perfectly safe here in bed. I keep telling myself this over and over again, but my hands are still shaking.

What was up with that dream? I had one almost just like it last year after I faced the Sprinter. I didn't understand it then and I don't get it now. I'm practically positive that I was a dove in the dream because I am Silver Dove, and I'm guessing that the crow in my dream is supposed to be the Crow. If that is true, then why were we so friendly with each other? We hate each other. In the dream I felt that the crow in it was both my enemy and my friend. The Crow in real life is just my enemy, and a very stubborn, pain in the butt enemy at that. In the dream though, we seemed very close, as if we truly are friends. And what about that strange creature that attacked us? What on earth is that supposed to be? I couldn't see it since it was covered in shadows, but I also had the same feelings toward it as I did for the crow. Why was I both afraid and drawn toward that thing?

I press my face into my pillow and groan. I can't let this stuff make me lose any sleep. I will never be able to figure it out. I mean it's a dream, it's not like it's telling me the future. At least I hope not. Closing my eyes and cuddling under my covers, I try to go back to sleep but rest evades me for the moment.

Something tells me though that my mind is trying to tell me something with that dream, to warn me about something that may happen. I don't know what it is, but if that massive creature is what I'm supposed to be worried about, then I know that things are about to get so much worse and I'm not sure if I can handle it.

Chapter Twenty- Two
Luis-
The Doctor

Colomba and I sit in the waiting room in the office of the doctor who ordered my painting. It is a very bland room. Off-white walls surround a room that is practically filled with black chairs placed in rows in front of the receptionist's desk. I now understand why the doctor wanted to order a painting for this room, I would go crazy with boredom if I was stuck waiting here in this dull room for too long. Right now, we are waiting for the doctor to be done with his final patient so that he can see the finished painting I now hold in my hands. The painting is wrapped in cloth to make sure that nothing gets on it. I'm glad that I have the cloth on it or else the sweat from my hands would be all over the painting by now. My stomach is churning in my nervousness and I'm afraid that I might throw up. If Colomba wasn't sitting beside me I may have already done that by now.

I stare ahead at the door that leads to the examination room, where I know the doctor is currently in. I almost beg the little hands on the clock to move faster so that I can get this over with. He's going to hate it. I just know that he will. Why did he even ask me to do this painting for him?

Colomba must have noticed how nervous I am since she gently rests her hand on top of mine. I look over at her in surprise, and she just gives me a simple, reassuring smile. I smile back at her as the two of us silently wait. I know what she meant by holding my hand like that, she was telling me that it will be alright, I am with you.

Another minute passes before the doctor and his final patient come out of the examination room. The doctor and his patient exchange a simple farewell before the patient walks out the door and the doctor turns his attention to me.

He is a rather short man with a large belly. Wire glasses are perched on his long nose and a shining scalp is starting to be seen from his thinning, black hair. His eyes are thin and dark, but I see friendliness within them that makes his entire face light up. When you look at him, you can't help but feel better because joy just seems to come from this man, like warmth from a fire. A huge smile is on his face as he walks up to Colomba and I. We both stand up as he extends his hand for us to shake.

"Good afternoon, good afternoon children. I am so glad that you could make it today. I have been very anxious to see this painting of yours Luis." He looks over at Colomba with undeniable kindness.

"And you must be the model he used for this painting. I recognize you from his portrait from the fair. I must admit that I can understand why he was so eager to have you pose for him. You are a very lovely girl." Colomba lowers her head as a smile plays across her lips and a blush forms on her cheeks. Judging from how embarrassed I feel by his comment, I'm probably blushing too.

"Now let's see this amazing painting." The doctor says with enthusiasm.

"Of course, Dr. Huang." I gently pull the cloth off of the painting and hold it up for him to see. He leans forward to examine it closely. I look down at it to see my work. The painting shows Colomba in a pale blue dress with her dark hair pulled back in a ponytail using a dark blue ribbon. In the painting she is sitting on a rock on the edge of the lake in the park, her feet are dangling right over the water. She is looking down at her feet, as if she sees something swimming close to her feet and is slightly curious about it. A small, contented smile is on her lips as she enjoys the peaceful place around her. The scene is so realistic that you can almost hear the wind blowing through the trees above her, gently rustling the leaves. As I watch him stare at the painting, my heart seems to fall in my chest. He hates it, he really hates it. I look away from him, not wanting to see the look of disappointment on his face when he tells me that he won't pay me for a piece of junk like this. I wait for the crushing words, but I am surprised when I hear a gasp of excitement.

"This has to be one of the best paintings I have seen in my whole life!" I look back up at him with wide eyes. Did he really just say that? Does he really think it's that good? When I look at his face, I can tell that he's telling me the truth. The doctor's eyes glow with wonder, like a child looking in the window of a candy store.

"You really like it?" He finally looks away from the painting to glance up at me as if I am being silly.

"Like it? I love this! It is beautiful!" I feel something on my shoulder, I glance over to my side to see Colomba resting her hand on my shoulder. She is smiling up at me with pride and joy. My disbelief seems to melt away as I look at her smile. I did it, I actually did it. I actually got paid for one of my paintings. Someone actually thinks that I made something worthwhile. The doctor hands me a check to pay for the painting while I hand him my masterpiece.

Colomba and I walk out the front door together, both of us still smiling. Dr. Huang's office is right in the middle of downtown, I can actually see my uncle's shop from where we are standing, only about five shopfronts down. I hold the check in my hand, still surprised that I have it. The doctor gave me three hundred dollars for that painting. I'm so grateful that he paid me so much. I've never really had that much money to call my own. My parents left behind some money for me after they died, but I won't get that until I'm eighteen. I would rather have the money now, it kinda sucks, but I have to deal with it until my eighteenth birthday. I suppose I can survive without it until then. It is nice to know that when I become an adult and move out of my uncle's place, I will have some money to help me out.

My heart swells with happiness when I

look down at Colomba beside me. In my heart, I feel as if she is responsible for how well I did with that painting. Since she was in it, I worked harder since I wanted to capture how perfect she is to me. I want anyone who sees that painting to know how perfect she is. I clear my throat awkwardly as I build up my courage to do what I have been wanting to do since I met her. I'm finally going to ask her out on a date.

"Umm Colomba?"

"Yes Luis." She smiles at me and I have to force myself to focus so that I can keep talking without tripping over my words.

"Well, if you don't have anything else to do today… since you were kind enough to help me out with the painting do- do you think that maybe we can-?"

"Hey you two, how's it going?!" I turn around with rage boiling in me as I look at the one person I wanted the most to not be around me today, Alex. I quickly hide the check in my pocket. I didn't even think about doing that, it just came naturally. After all the years of torture I've had with Alex, I just know that if I have something that I like then I should hide it or else he might take it or destroy it.

He isn't even really looking at me, all of his attention is directed at Colomba. Alex is smiling at her as if they are very close. I smile to myself as I see this. She's just going to brush him off like before. I'm going to enjoy watching this. I glance down at Colomba, expecting her to be scowling at him. I'm surprised to see that she is smiling back at him. Why on earth is she smiling at him? After everything that happened at the fair over the summer, and the way she's been treating him recently, I thought that she would hate him right now.

"Hello Alex, how are you?" Her voice is friendly, and she is looking at him as if she has no anger toward him at all even though she was looking at him like he was a disgusting bug just the other day. What is going on here?

"Doing good. What are you guys up to?" He glances over at me and sneers at me before he looks back at Colomba with his usual confident grin.

"We were just dropping off Luis' painting that he did for Dr. Huang. It looked really fantastic, he's such an amazing artist." She smiles at me with pride while Alex glares at me for a split second.

"I bet he is. Let's face it though, it would be impossible for a painting to look bad if a pretty girl like you is in it." Colomba looks uncomfortable for a minute at his compliment before her smile returns, although it seems a bit halfhearted now.

"Thanks Alex, that's very sweet of you to say." He gives her a confident wink and I see her blink rapidly in surprise at how daring he was to do that.

"I'm actually really glad that I bumped into you. I found out not too long ago the score I got on the math test you helped me with." He falls silent and I know that he is trying to lure her farther into the conversation by making her ask him about it, and she falls for it.

"How did you do Alex?"

"I got a C, that's the best I've done on a test all year. Are you proud of me?" Jeez, that's the best this guy has done all year? My Uncle Diego would kill me if I got grades like that. Colomba on the other hand, smiles at him as if this is some major accomplishment.

"That's fantastic. Great job Alex. I am very proud of you." His already large grin just seems to grow even bigger when he hears her praise him. My fists are so tight that my fingernails are digging into my palms and they are screaming with pain. Even though I know that I will make my hands bleed if I keep this up, I don't loosen my grip. I am too angry to do that.

"How about we celebrate? Since you were so sweet and helped tutor me, how about I buy you lunch? The Captain's Ship is just around the corner, I can buy you a burger." He gives her a look that I know far too well from knowing him so long. He always has this certain devious, yet somehow charming, look in his eyes whenever he is flirting with a girl and he is giving that look full force to Colomba now. She glances away from him, not looking even remotely flattered by his attention like how most girls are when he uses that look on them. She is silent for a moment before a sudden idea seems to spark in her mind and a smile appears on her lips as she turns her attention to me.

"How about you come with us Luis? We can celebrate you selling your first painting too. I would be happy to pay for you since this is your accomplishment." She smiles at me hopefully and I instantly understand what's going on. She doesn't want to be rude and refuse Alex's invitation, but she also doesn't want to be alone with him. She wants me to be almost like a chaperone. She wants me to watch over her and protect her from Alex. That I am happy to do.

"Sure, that sounds like fun. You don't have to pay for me though. With the money I earned, I'm set." I glare at Alex who glares back at me for an instant before he smiles down at Colomba.

"Alright, if we're going to go, let's go." Under the friendliness of his words, I detect a faint growl in his voice. He marches ahead of us, his feet stomping on the sidewalk. Colomba smiles up at me and I understand her silent message. She's thanking me for coming along. I smile back at her, sending her my own silent message, telling her that I am happy to be with her.

We follow Alex around the corner and walk right into the Captain's Ship. The three of us sit in a booth, but I make sure that I am sitting beside Colomba, making Alex sit across from us instead. He sits down, looking very disappointed that he didn't get to sit beside her and that he's stuck with me tagging along on what he had obviously hoped would be a date. An entire minute of awkward silence falls between the three of us before the waitress takes our order. I order a burger and fries, Colomba orders a chocolate milkshake, while Alex orders a large soda, three burgers, and a large fry. Colomba looks at Alex with confusion, hearing him order so much food. Alex just smiles at her with amusement.

"More muscle means I need to have more

food." To emphasize his words, he raises one arm to flex his muscles, showing off a ripped bicep. I look away, suddenly feeling embarrassed by how weak I am compared to him. Colomba glances away from him too, embarrassed as well by him showing off. She turns her attention to me instead, her bright smile returning.

"Dr. Huang looked so pleased with your painting. I'm so happy for you, you did so well. It looked like a professional painting, like something that you would put in a museum." I smile back at her, both of us completely ignoring Alex.

"One day, I hope that I can get something in a museum, or even a gallery. That's kind of my dream right now."

"I know that you'll make it one day. You're too good of an artist to get anything less." The two of us just smile at each other while I watch Alex's face grow red in fury from the corner of my eye. I have to keep myself from laughing at the sight of him. His head is so red that it looks like a tomato that has been glued to the top of his body. He clears his throat to get our attention back on him. Colomba looks over at him, but she doesn't seem interested.

"Do you think that you'll still be able to be my tutor the rest of the year? I know that with your help I can make it through." He smiles at her again, trying to lay on the charm, but Colomba isn't falling for it. She just gives him a very serious reply.

"Well I've been assigned to work with you, so you're stuck with me until either the year is over, or you get good enough grades that the teacher in charge of the tutoring program says that you don't need me anymore." Alex just smiles even wider.

"Well then, I'll just have to make sure that my grades stay terrible so that I'll still be able to see you so often." Even though what he's saying seems ridiculous, it is obvious from his tone that he is serious. Colomba's eyes grow wide in surprise while mine narrow in disgust. This guy is going to let his grades suffer just to hang out with a girl? I'm the guy who has never had a girlfriend, and I still find that pretty pathetic.

It looks as if Colomba plans on saying something to Alex about what he just said, probably to tell him that's stupid, but the waitress interrupts her. She places our food in front of us while an uncomfortable silence falls over the three of us again. I start eating some of my fries while Colomba sips her milkshake, making sure not to look at either of us. Alex doesn't seem to realize how uncomfortable Colomba and I are right now, he just starts talking like everything is normal with this situation. I pick up one of my fries to take a bite, but the fry stops in midair when I hear what Alex says.

"You know when I was... doing that stuff for the Crow," I have to smile since I know that he was trying to avoid saying that he was controlled by me, "he was such a creep. He ordered me around like I was his dog or something." He shakes his head as if what happened was ridiculous when I know that he was terrified. I read every thought in his head, I could feel his fear. His brows furrow in confusion as a thought seems to pass through that tiny mind of his. "There was something strange about the Crow though." This seems to grab

Colomba's attention since she finally glances up from the table to stare at him intently.

"What about him was strange?" Usually Alex would be smiling when he notices that he has Colomba's attention, but he seems to be stuck in his own head, thinking about his experience with me.

"It was his voice. There was something about that voice of his in my head, it almost sounded," he looks over at me, closely examining my face as if he is trying to find something, "familiar." The fry drops from my hand and back on my plate. I can no longer hear the soft rock music that is playing in the background. As silence falls between the three of us, I hear my blood pounding in my ears. He stares at me for what feels like eternity. No, no, no, no, no, no, *no*! He can't figure this out! He just can't! The two of us just glare at each other for an entire minute in silence while Colomba stares at the two of us in confusion. As I look in his eyes, I can only think one thing, don't say anything. Don't say what you're thinking out loud. Don't you even dare try to tell her who I really am. If you do then you will regret the moment you were born.

Alex scoffs and starts smiling again as if the last three tense minutes didn't happen.

"Of course, that would be impossible. I would know who the Crow was if I could recognize his voice. He thinks that he's so smart, but if I had even the slightest hint, I would find out who he is and make sure that he wouldn't hurt anybody again." I have to control myself to make sure that I don't let my relief show. I also have to make sure that I don't show my annoyance either. This guy thinks that he will make sure that I won't hurt anybody again? That guy was almost peeing in his pants in terror every time I spoke in his head when I possessed him. If I showed up right now in my Crow form, I know that he would run away to protect himself. He wouldn't bother to try and help anybody else because he is secretly a coward. I know that now because I was in his mind when I transformed him. He is just trying to make himself sound like a hero in front of Colomba though, trying to impress her. It doesn't seem to be working. She just nods her head at that comment and sips her milkshake, obviously bored with what he's saying now that he isn't going to say who the voice reminded him of.

I smile at her, trying to get rid of the tension that Alex created with his comment.

"Don't worry, the Crow has never really hurt anybody, just scared a bunch of people. I don't think that he really wants to hurt anybody at all. He's just trying to teach everyone a lesson, that's it." Alex chuckles.

"Yeah, but if he ever does go completely nuts and tries to hurt you Colomba, I'll be here to protect you." She doesn't even look at him as he tells her that, and my smile just gets bigger as I speak again.

"And I'll be here too. I won't let anyone hurt you or any of my friends. I will do whatever it takes to keep you guys safe." Colomba smiles at me, completely ignoring Alex. I don't look at him, but I know that he has noticed this and is glaring at me. I can feel the hate coming from him that is making my stomach churn in fear, almost making me so nervous that I'll throw up, but I won't look at him. I won't give him the satisfaction of knowing that he is scaring me right now. Today I have won. Colomba may be acting nice to him again for some reason, but she doesn't really care about him and he knows it. I am the only one that she has really paid attention to. I have won against Alex for now, and I let myself enjoy it as I go through everything that happened when I transformed him. I relive every second that I felt his fear toward me. After being afraid of him for so long, it felt nice to have him be scared of me instead. It felt nice to have that power. When I drew a picture of him as the Bull-Y in my sketchbook last night, I felt that power rising in me with every stroke of my pencil. I made sure to give him that same stupid stare he had when I transformed him. That's how I always want to remember him as, the big, stupid monster.

Colomba tries to start a conversation between the three of us, but Alex and I are not very interested in it. The two of us are too busy sending silent messages to each other. We are both sending the exact message. I hate you, and I will make you more miserable than you have ever been. I will make sure of that.

Don't miss the previous books in The Adventures of Silver Dove series.

Eliza Scalia is a therapist who has a master's degree in Clinical Mental Health from Troy University. She enjoys reading, writing, and needlework, as well as hanging out with her pet cat, Dusty. Eliza has been writing since she was in middle school and has self- published the Death's Assistant series for young adults.

www.ingramcontent.com/pod-product-compliance
Lightning Source LLC
Chambersburg PA
CBHW070513200726
48293CB00007B/2515